ZUCCHINI

Also by Barbara Dana

RUTGERS AND THE WATER SNOUTS

CRAZY EIGHTS

ZUCCHINI

Barbara Dana

drawings by Eileen Christelow

1 8 1 7

HARPER & ROW, PUBLISHERS

Cambridge, Philadelphia, San Francisco, London, Mexico City, São Paulo, Sydney

NEW YORK

Zucchini

 Printed in the United States of America. For information address Harper & Row, Publishers, Inc., 10 East 53rd Street, New York, N.Y. 10022. Published simultaneously in Canada by Fitzhenry & Whiteside Limited, Toronto.
First Edition

Library of Congress Cataloging in Publication Data
Dana, Barbara.
Zucchini.

"A Charlotte Zolotow book"–Half t.p.
Summary: A painfully shy young boy befriends a homeless baby ferret and gets as much comfort as he gives.
[1. Friendship–Fiction. 2. Bashfulness–Fiction. 3. Ferrets–Fiction] I. Christelow, Eileen, ill. II. Title.
PZ7.D188Zu 1982 [Fic] 80-8448
ISBN 0-06-021394-9 AACR2
ISBN 0-06-021395-7 (lib. bdg.)

To my beloved Guru,
Hari,
and my beloved Paramguru,
Ralph Harris Houston

Chapter One

Some Kind of Weasel

Zucchini was born in the rodent house at the Bronx Zoo. When he was six weeks old, the rodent man put him in a cage of his own, separating him from his mother. It was time for him to become independent.

For days, the tiny ferret huddled in the corner of his glass-enclosed cage, refusing to eat. He wanted nothing but his mother. He would wait for her return. The zoo people had placed her at the far end of the rodent house, but noting Zucchini's condition after three days, had moved her to a cage directly across from her offspring. Zucchini picked up his mother's scent instantly and moved to the front of his cage. He peered questioningly through the thickness of the glass that separated them.

"You'll do well," his mother told him with her eyes. "You're growing up. It's time to become independent."

"I don't want to be independent," said Zucchini. "I want to be with you."

"Be patient," said his mother. "That will change."

As the days passed, Zucchini began to feel more comfortable. After all, there wasn't much that could happen to him in his tiny cage with its orange light and fake ground. No need to panic.

He could survive. Then on the seventh day, his mother was again moved to the far end of the rodent house.

I'll be all right, thought Zucchini, but still he was lonely. He had no one. No brothers or sisters, no friends of any kind. The cage on his left was empty, and the one on his right had bats. Zucchini didn't like bats. He could hear them endlessly flapping around, banging into the walls, and he couldn't figure out what they were after.

Across the way lived a Mexican pocket gopher and a restless groundhog. The pocket gopher spent her time tunneling through an elaborate network of passageways while the groundhog paced. Zucchini could sense that they both would rather not be interrupted, so he left them alone.

Sometimes Zucchini would catch a glimpse of the rodent man. His name was Rex, and he wore a faded green uniform. Mostly, Rex would stand around, leaning on his shovel, staring into space. Zucchini often wondered why Rex had a shovel. (There wasn't anything to dig.)

Zucchini passed his days in boredom. The big event of the day was when Rex dropped a carrot into his cage and gave him fresh water. Sometimes Zucchini would try to think up new activities, but the possibilities were few. He could walk in circles, back up, take a nap, eat, clean his fur, make up stories, drink his water or hide inside his log from the people who looked into his cage.

Every day people would come and peer at Zucchini through the glass and point their fingers.

"What's that?" someone would usually ask.

"Beats me," another would answer. "Must be some kind of weasel."

"What kind of weasel?"

"Beats me."

Each day the people would mutter in confusion because the rodent house was dark, and Zucchini's sign was poorly lit. Also, some of the letters had come off. The people who took the trouble to bend, squint, put on their glasses or get out their flashlights only came up with F RR T ZUCC NI, which wasn't a lot of help. Rex noted the confusion with a wry smile and silently cursed the maintenance department. Those guys never get things done, was his feeling.

Zucchini adjusted to his surroundings, but deep down he felt there must be more to life. At night he would sometimes dream of open places, places with light and air and different smells and beautiful colors, but when he woke up he could barely remember.

Where was I? he would think. Was it real? It was nice. Not like here. What is this place? So dark and cramped and pointless. Is this where I belong? I'm so lonely. I'm not having a good time, and I'm not doing anybody else any good. Something's wrong.

These feelings built up in Zucchini until he had no choice but to share them.

I'll try the groundhog, he thought. I'll interrupt him for once. This is important.

Zucchini waited until nighttime, when the rodent house was quiet and free of people.

"Excuse me," he said in a somewhat timid voice to the pacing groundhog. "Could I speak to you for a minute?"

"Suit yourself," said the groundhog.

"I'm sorry to bother you. I know you're busy, but I'm young and tiny and you're older and you seem to have things organized."

"Get to the point," said the groundhog.

"Yes," said Zucchini. "Well, I've been wondering about something."

"That's your first mistake," said the groundhog.

"What's that?"

"Wondering. It'll get you nowhere."

"I don't do it on purpose," said Zucchini.

"Well, stop," said the groundhog. "One, two, three. Where's your willpower?"

"I don't have any," said Zucchini.

"Rubbish," said the groundhog.

Zucchini waited a moment, then gathered his courage.

"Do you ever get the feeling there's more?"

"More what?" said the groundhog. He was circling his rock, heading back in the direction of his water bowl.

"More things," said Zucchini, "more than we see. This rodent house, the cages, the orange lights, the water bowls, the rocks, the bats, the people staring in at us, Rex—is that all there is?"

"What you see is what you get," said the groundhog.

"At night I see other places, places with light and air and different smells and beautiful colors."

"You're dreaming," said the groundhog. "It's all in the mind."

Zucchini thought about what the groundhog had told him, but could make no sense of it.

It's all in the mind, he thought, but is that the only place it is? Maybe it's in the mind and also in other places. It's all in the mind means that everything is in the mind, but isn't everything also everywhere else? I should have asked him. He didn't make it clear.

Chapter Two

Shrew's Tale

The next day, a new arrival was brought in. It was a tiny masked shrew, and Rex placed her in the empty cage on Zucchini's left. The shrew slept for several hours, then woke up, blinked her eyes and began backing up. Zucchini's cage was at a slight right angle to the shrew's cage, so he had a good view of the goings-on. He watched as the shrew circled her cage several times backward, bashed into the wall, fell over, got up, reversed direction and ran, full speed ahead, toward a metal drain on the floor of her cage. When she reached the drain she began digging furiously.

Zucchini moved up to his window and stared in disbelief. "What are you doing?" he asked.

"Digging," said the shrew.

"I see that," said Zucchini, "but why?"

"I have to get back," said the shrew. She didn't stop digging. Scratch, scratch, scratch, went her tiny nails on the hard cement surface.

"Back where?" said Zucchini.

"Back home," said the shrew.

"Where's home?" asked Zucchini.

"Dutchess County," said the shrew. "My nest is all set up. Dried leaves and grass. It's perfect."

"Well, where is that?" asked Zucchini. "Where is Dutchess County?"

"Can't talk," said the shrew. "No time."

"Oh, please," said Zucchini. "Don't tell me that! This is important! The groundhog says there is no other place. He says this rodent house is all there is, but I don't believe him."

"No time," said the shrew. "Sorry for the inconvenience."

"It's no inconvenience," said Zucchini. "It's my life! Stop digging! Please! Listen! Just answer one question! Answer this question, and I promise I won't ask any more!"

The shrew stopped digging and stared at Zucchini with piercing eyes. "Just one," said the shrew.

"Just one," said Zucchini.

"What is it?" said the shrew.

Zucchini took a deep breath. "Is Dutchess County in this rodent house?"

"No," said the shrew.

"No!" said Zucchini.

"That'll be all," said the shrew. She turned back to the drain and resumed digging with purpose.

"I knew it," said Zucchini. "There is somewhere else!"

That night Zucchini returned to the groundhog. "It's me again," he said, peering through the darkness of the rodent house.

"What now?" said the groundhog. He was standing in his water bowl, presumably soaking his paws.

"That shrew over there," said Zucchini, "she's been digging for hours. Have you noticed?"

"I've noticed," said the groundhog.

"I asked her about it, and she said she wants to get back. She belongs in Dutchess County. She has a nest set up and everything."

"So what?" said the groundhog.

"Well, where is that?" said Zucchini. "I never heard of it."

"Are you king of the world?"

"No."

"Well, there you are."

Zucchini thought about that for a minute while the groundhog stepped slowly out of his water bowl and shook the water from his paws.

"Excuse me for continuing," said Zucchini, "but what does that have to do with anything?"

"Nothing," said the groundhog.

"Well, why did you mention it?"

"Two can play that game."

"What game?" said Zucchini.

"What you've heard of doesn't have anything to do with anything either," said the groundhog. "It's got no bearing."

"What I mean," said Zucchini, "is that if Dutchess County is a place I never heard of, then it might be a place you never heard of; and if it's real and it's not here, then it must be somewhere else. Do you see what I'm driving at?"

"Not really," said the groundhog. He began pacing again, back and forth along the edge of his glass window.

"Stop pacing!" said Zucchini. "Listen! The shrew says there's more!"

The groundhog stopped and stared at Zucchini as if he'd gone mad. "Are you going to listen to a shrew?" he asked. "Look at the size of her. Consider her brain. Like a pea, or smaller. You decide."

"I guess I'll have to," said Zucchini. He watched as the groundhog resumed his pacing. "Can I ask one more question?"

"Make it brief," said the groundhog.

"Where do the people go?"

"What people?"

"The people who come in here," said Zucchini. "They go up those stairs and disappear. Where do they go?"

"They're people," said the groundhog. "They've got their ways."

"But if they go somewhere, that means there's somewhere to go."

"If you want to follow a bunch of lunatic people, that's your business."

Zucchini couldn't help feeling that the groundhog was hiding something. He watched him pace and sensed his restlessness.

"Do you like it here?" Zucchini asked.

"I hate it," said the groundhog, "but the food is regular."

Chapter Three

Letter

The next morning a noisy group of third graders woke Zucchini up, shouting and jumping around.

What's this? thought Zucchini as he peered out from inside his hollow log.

"Quiet!" the teacher was saying. "Turn your attention here." She looked exhausted and was sipping coffee from a plastic no-spill thermos.

"What's that?" said a large boy in a torn T-shirt. He was pointing at Zucchini.

"That's a ferret," said the teacher. "We spoke of them in class, you may recall."

"I don't recall nothin'," said the boy. "Not me." He went over to the bats and pounded on the glass window. *"HOO, HOO,"* he shrieked.

I wish he wouldn't do that, thought Zucchini. He crawled back into his log and put his paws over his ears.

"HOO, HOO," shrieked the boy.

"Stop that, Bruce," said the teacher. "Stop that this minute, or you will sit on the bus."

The boy sat down on the floor and stared at his knees.

"This way," said the teacher. "We're due at the birds at eleven." She took a last long sip of coffee and led the children up the stairs.

The boy remained motionless.

"Off the floor," shouted Rex. He was down by the kangaroo rats, leaning on his shovel. "Off the floor. Follow your group."

The boy remained on the floor, still staring at his knees. Rex set his shovel up against the wall and moved up to the boy. Next to him stood a small dark-haired girl who looked quietly at Zucchini.

"Move it, now. Both of ya," said Rex. "You'll get lost in this place."

"I won't get lost," said the girl. "I know where the birds are, and I have a watch." She pulled a neatly folded piece of paper from her pocket. "Will you give this to the ferret?" she asked.

"What is it?" said Rex.

"It's a letter," said the girl. "I'd do it myself, but I can't get into his cage. You have a key."

"There's no key," said Rex. "Now beat it." He turned to the boy. "You too. Off the floor."

"Why won't you give it to him?" said the girl. She was almost in tears.

"Ferrets can't read," said Rex.

"How do you know?" asked the girl.

"Anybody knows," said Rex.

"They understand more than you think," said the girl.

"Sure they do. Right. They understand more than you think, but they can't read."

"You don't know that," the girl insisted. "You just think it in your big mind, but maybe you're wrong."

"Beat it," said Rex.

"Please," said the girl. She began to cry. "I worked so hard. It took me three whole hours."

"All right. Don't cry," said Rex. "Give it to me." He reached out for the letter. "Give it to me and get out of here."

"Thank you," said the girl. She gave Rex the letter and turned to the boy. "It's almost eleven," she said.

The boy got up slowly and followed her up the stairs to find the others.

Rex stuffed the letter in his pocket and forgot about it until late that afternoon. It had been a quiet day, and Rex was bored. He reached into his pocket for a pack of Velamints he remembered having left there, pulled out the mints and also the letter.

"Oh, yeah," he muttered to himself. He popped a Velamint into his mouth and approached Zucchini's cage. "You got a letter," he said.

Zucchini crawled out from inside his log.

What's a letter? he thought.

If Rex hadn't been so bored he never would have read the letter, but standing around the darkened rodent house on a quiet day was a kind of torture for Rex. By three o'clock he was ready for anything. He moved up near Zucchini's window. "Get this now," he said.

After years in the rodent house Rex's eyes had become accustomed to the darkness. He had little trouble making out the letters as he read:

Dear Ferret,

How are you? I am calling you Ferret because I don't know what your name is because your sign is all messed up. I am interested in animals that are dissappearing and one of them is you the black-footed ferret.

My teacher says that you are indangered. I am sorry for that. I wish I knew more about you. I know you come from the open prairys where the land is flat. I know thats near Oklahoma because my ant lives there but I don't know anything else. I am 8. I wish I was older so I could stop you from being indangered. But that job is for grown ups. Do you like it in this zoo? I wouldn't.

Your friend,
Cindy Marco

"That's your mail for today," said Rex in a sarcastic tone. Then he tore up the letter and threw it in the trash.

Zucchini's heart pounded in his tiny chest.

The open prairies! That's it! That's where I came from! That's where I belong!

That night Zucchini planned his escape. He huddled in the corner of his cage, shivering from nervousness.

I'll leave tomorrow, he thought. The sooner, the better. I'll leave when Rex gives me my carrot. He always opens my door pretty wide when he gives me that carrot. If I move fast I can make it. I'll leave my cage, and I'll run up those stairs. That's where the people go. The groundhog says that people have their ways, but if one of their ways is getting out of this rodent house then that's for me. I'll run up those stairs, and no matter what I see when I get to the top, I'll keep going.

Zucchini paced awhile from nervousness, then settled down and tried to sleep. As usual, he covered his eyes with his tiny paws because his orange light was always left on, and it kept him awake.

What am I doing? he thought. I'm planning a daring escape that will never work, to a place I've never been. Maybe there is no such place. Maybe there's nothing out there at all. Maybe it's cold and black, or empty, or just like here. Maybe upstairs is another rodent house with another Rex, or more of this very same rodent house. I could get hurt, or die, or starve. Maybe they don't have any grain, or water, or carrots. I'd miss carrots. Maybe I should wait. I'm not full grown. I'm small, and I don't know much. I should be strong and wise for such a trip.

But something told Zucchini that if he waited he'd never leave. He'd be in the rodent house forever. He'd get old and lose his courage. He'd become like the groundhog and close his mind.

It's now or never, he said to himself. It's up to me.

He lay huddled inside his log and listened to the shrew scratching away at the drain and the bats banging into the walls and the groundhog pacing back and forth until, in an anxious state, he fell asleep.

Chapter Four

Escape

When Zucchini woke up, a lady in a hat was pointing at him and instructing a group of children to check off domestic weasel.

"Check off domestic weasel," she was saying. "Check him off. This weasel is sleeping."

She's mixed up, thought Zucchini. I'm a ferret, and I'm awake.

Then he remembered.

Today was the day!

His heart began to pound, and he felt dizzy.

Rex usually changed Zucchini's water at four o'clock. By three Zucchini was already in position. At first he had thought of pretending to be asleep when Rex opened his cage, but he had decided against that.

I never sleep when Rex gives me my carrot, he thought. If Rex finds me asleep, he might suspect something. I don't want that.

So Zucchini decided to sit in the corner with his regular look of eager anticipation and readiness, and trust that Rex would think it was eager anticipation and readiness for his carrot, and not eager anticipation and readiness to escape.

Three-fifteen, three-thirty, three-forty-five.

Zucchini's heart pounded harder and harder as he took his position in the corner. At five minutes past four Rex opened the door of Zucchini's cage. Zucchini felt his heart leap up into his throat. Rex reached for the water dish and Zucchini made his dash.

"Hey, wait a minute," said Rex, dropping the water dish.

Off toward the stairs dashed Zucchini. He passed his mother's cage with his mother asleep inside. He wanted to say good-bye, but there was no time. Rex was close behind. Up the stairs he ran as fast as he could. Rex was gaining on him.

Faster, legs! thought Zucchini. Take me faster!

When he reached the top of the stairs, Zucchini felt his heart stop. At the top of the stairs was a door. And the door was shut.

Oh, no! thought Zucchini, but the door swung open and a group of children started through.

"Move, move," shouted Rex, pushing the children to one side. "Sorry, sorry."

Zucchini scurried around the feet of the children and out into the sunlight.

How beautiful, he thought. There's a whole world out here!

He hurried down the path, past the buffalo, toward the elephants.

What are those things? he thought, but he had no time to stop.

Down the path followed Rex.

"Ferret loose!" Rex shouted, but nobody seemed to care.

Zucchini was tiring fast. He had never run before, never in his life, and his muscles were weak. He tried to run faster, pushing himself almost beyond his limit, but Rex was gaining fast.

"Stop that ferret!" shouted Rex.

Zucchini could see the crowd of people by the front gate. It was almost closing time, and they were milling around, collecting themselves.

Better not go that way, he thought. Somebody might step on me, or grab me by the tail.

By the side of the gate was a fence. Zucchini dove headfirst through one of the spaces in the mesh. It was a tight squeeze.

I'm not going to make this, he thought. I'm stuck!

"Grab him!" shouted Rex.

Zucchini summoned all his strength. He dug his tiny nails into the ground and pulled. He pulled and pulled and at last he was free, safe on the other side!

"Dumb ferret," said Rex.

"Look at the squirrel running funny like that," said a little girl, pointing in Zucchini's direction.

"That's not a squirrel," said the father.

"What is it?" asked the girl.

"Something else," the father answered with authority.

Zucchini headed down 180th Street and soon came upon the IRT subway, which at this location was raised on tracks high above the street. Above his head a train came to a screeching halt. Zucchini had never seen a train before, but it moved fast and speed was what he needed. Up the flight of stairs he dashed and under the turnstile to the waiting train. The doors slammed shut behind him, the train started up and Zucchini sat on the floor of an IRT subway car, blinking in the bright fluorescent light.

Chapter Five

Squirrel on the IRT

There were several passengers in Zucchini's car, but for the first few minutes no one looked his way. Then a lady with a large shopping bag, wearing three sweaters and a brown hat, turned to the boy next to her.

"Since when do they have squirrels?" she said, poking the boy hard in the ribs.

"I don't know," said the boy. His mind was elsewhere.

Then the lady shouted across to a small man who didn't have any teeth.

"Now they got squirrels," she said, jerking her head toward Zucchini.

"What?" said the man. He leaned forward and squinted his eyes. "I can't hear you."

"What'll be next?" said the woman. She was chuckling to herself now.

"Simpson Street," said the man, shouting over the noise of the train. His face was all red from the exertion.

"I said squirrels, what's next?" shouted the woman.

The man shook his head and went back to the book he was reading. Then the woman went over to the man and shouted in his ear.

"There's a squirrel on this train," she said.

The man looked at Zucchini, nodded at the woman and went back to his book. Zucchini put his paws over his ears.

He was unaccustomed to such noise, and his ears had begun to ache. Then the train entered its underground tunnel. Outside the windows it was suddenly pitch-black.

Where are we? thought Zucchini. I don't like this.

When the train stopped at Ninety-sixth Street, the doors opened, and Zucchini followed a group of people off the train.

Let me out of here, he thought. This is worse than the rodent house.

He followed the crowd down and then up the stairs and out onto the street. It was cloudy, but the sun peeked through the clouds and Zucchini caught a glimpse of blue sky.

How beautiful, he thought.

There was a large group of people on the corner, waiting to board the crosstown bus. Zucchini stopped for a moment to rest. He took several deep breaths. Tired as he was, it was good to be out of his cage, free at last.

That groundhog was so wrong, thought Zucchini. As wrong as he could be.

A large bus pulled to a stop and people began getting on.

I'll try this, thought Zucchini. It's quieter than that long screeching thing and faster than my feet.

He waited his turn and climbed the two enormous steps toward the driver.

"Hold on there a minute," said the driver from under his cap. "Where do you think you're going?"

Why is he shouting at me? thought Zucchini.

"No squirrels," said the driver. "Off the bus."

"But he's so cute," said a small lady wearing a hat with a veil.

"That's got nothing to do with it," said the driver.

"Come with me," said the lady. She bent down and picked up Zucchini.

"No one rides for free," said the driver. "Only babies."

"Then I'll pay for him," said the lady, and she reached into her purse, took out some change and dropped it into the coin box.

By this time a lot of people were getting impatient and were shouting things like "What's going on here?" "Let's go" and "Move it!"

"All right, all right," said the driver, pushing his cap back on his head. "What do I care? She wants squirrels, she gets squirrels." He glanced in his rearview mirror, pulled the lever to shut the doors and started up the bus. "It takes all kinds," he said.

The lady found a seat and sat, holding Zucchini close.

"Where'd you find him?" The man in the next seat was peering cautiously down at Zucchini.

"He got on at Broadway," said the lady in a confidential tone. "I don't know where he's going, though."

"Probably crosstown," said the man, amused with himself.

"Oh, yes," the lady answered gravely.

The lady's lap was warm, and Zucchini was happy for the chance to rest.

"This is where I get off," she said suddenly, looking down at Zucchini. "Is that all right with you?"

Zucchini stared at the lady, wishing he could make her understand. He was comfortable for the first time, at least since the early times with his mother. Don't get up, he thought. Let's stay like this.

"Oh, dear," continued the lady. "Here we go."

When they got off the bus, the lady set Zucchini down on the sidewalk.

"I'd like to take you home," she said, "but my cats would never hear of it."

Zucchini gave the lady a thankful look and started off down Lexington Avenue.

The farther away from Rex, the better, he thought.

It was dark now and getting cold. Along Lexington Avenue different shops were closing for the night. A vacant-eyed man slammed shut the gate of Tillman Cleaners; two ladies peered into the register at Lucille's Lingerie; a square-shaped man in a green Windbreaker was locking up his hardware store. BETTER THINGS THROUGH HARDWARE, said the sign in the window. People hurried on their way to their homes, not one turning to notice the baby ferret, alone on Lexington Avenue. When Zucchini got to Eighty-seventh Street it began to rain.

What's this? he thought, shaking the dampness from his fur. I'd better find a place to hide.

He spotted a terrace on the second floor of a building on Eighty-seventh Street and made his way up a fire escape. The rain was falling heavily, and it was very dark. Zucchini inched his way along, unable to see. Suddenly, he slipped into the narrow rain gutter on the side of the terrace. He tried pulling himself out, his tiny nails scratching furiously on the wet metal, but he couldn't get a grip.

I can't get out, he thought. I'm going to drown!

Chapter Six

Rescue

When Mrs. Villard noticed the stoppage she wasted no time in calling the drain man.

"It's leaking right through my bedroom window," she said to the drain man when she finally got him on the phone. "My bedroom is flooded."

"Uh-huh," the drain man said absently.

"I have a flood," she went on. "Can you come right away?"

"Oh, no," said the drain man.

"What?" asked Mrs. Villard, hoping she'd heard him wrong.

"It's raining," said the drain man as if that settled everything.

"I know it's raining," said Mrs. Villard. She patted her short gray hair nervously. "That's why my bedroom's flooded." Then she shouted. "Can you come?"

"When it stops raining," said the drain man. "Then I'll be over. Maybe next week."

"This is serious," said Mrs. Villard. She was looking down at her new Red Cross shoes, which were soaked through, the toes beginning to curl. "Can you come, or should I call someone else?"

"I'll be by," said the drain man, and he hung up the phone.

The drain man showed up two hours later.

"You got a flood here," he informed Mrs. Villard as she led

him into her bedroom. "Your floor's all flooded."

"That's why I called you," said Mrs. Villard.

"This is awful," said the drain man.

He climbed out onto the terrace, and within minutes he was banging on the window, asking to be let in.

"You've got some kind of animal," he said, rain draining down from under his hair. He wore no hat or coat and didn't carry an umbrella. "Some kind of something. That's your trouble."

"What do you mean?" asked Mrs. Villard. She was holding a large pot filled with water.

"I don't know, a rat maybe. Some kind of animal's causing your stoppage."

"An animal?"

"That's what you got," said the man. "Some kind of animal. He's wedged right into your rain gutter. I think he's dead."

"Oh," said Mrs. Villard. "Can you get him out?"

"I ain't no veterinarian," said the drain man, packing up his tools.

Mrs. Villard set down her pot of water and thought. She had a sister in Queens who loved animals. Maybe she could help. Mrs. Villard remembered seeing ASPCA* magazines at her sister's house. They usually had pictures on the cover of smiling men rescuing animals from high places. She called up her sister, got the number of the ASPCA and called them up.

"I would like to report an animal in trouble," Mrs. Villard said to the man on the other end of the phone. "Some animal is caught in my rain gutter. He might be dead."

"We'll be right there," said the man.

A half an hour later two men appeared at Mrs. Villard's door. Each had on a yellow rain slicker and carried a ladder.

"Hello," said the taller of the two. "We're from the ASPCA. Understand you've got an animal in trouble."

**Short for the American Society for the Prevention of Cruelty to Animals*

"That's right," said Mrs. Villard. "He's out here." She led the two men into her bedroom and toward the terrace door. There was nearly an inch of water on the floor and Mrs. Villard had put on her slip-on rain boots.

"You've got a flood here," said one of the men.

"I know," said Mrs. Villard.

The two men went out onto the terrace and Mrs. Villard went into the kitchen to check on her frozen tuna casserole. She opened the oven and poked it with a fork, but it was still frozen solid. Then she went back into the bedroom and found the two men already inside. One was holding Zucchini, and they were both looking at him anxiously.

"Is he dead?" asked Mrs. Villard.

"Don't think so," said one of the men. "He's unconscious, chilled through, but he seems to be breathing."

"He's breathing, all right," said the other.

"What is it?" asked Mrs. Villard.

"I'd say it was a ferret," said one of the men, "but that's crazy. These kind are very rare, and anyway, what would a ferret be doing on Eighty-seventh Street?"

Mrs. Villard thanked the men and gave them a towel. They wrapped up Zucchini and left, taking him down the stairs, out into the truck and off to the Ninety-second Street ASPCA.

Chapter Seven

Trapped

When Zucchini woke up he found himself locked in a small cage.

Where am I? he thought, blinking in the harsh fluorescent light.

He felt dizzy and his legs shook when he tried to stand.

A cage! They put me in a cage!

He closed his eyes and tried to stop the spinning in his head.

Let this be a dream, he thought. Let me open my eyes and find I'm free, no cage to hold me.

But when he opened his eyes there he was, trapped, cramped in a boxlike cage. Thick wire mesh enclosed him on every side.

"The ferret's awake!"

It was Miss Venucchi, the dark-haired lab assistant, who called out to Dr. Merlin.

"Oho!" said Dr. Merlin. He was obviously pleased and headed toward Zucchini's cage, his unbuttoned white lab coat flapping as he moved. "Well, well, well."

Who are these people? thought Zucchini. Why are they staring at me? LET ME OUT!

"Looks pretty good," said Miss Venucchi, snapping her Chiclets gum as she spoke.

"Eyes aren't clear though," said Dr. Merlin. "Mm."

"Want me to take his temperature?"

"Better do that," said Dr. Merlin. "Then I'll look him over. Well, well, well."

Miss Venucchi took a firm grip on the latch and swung open the door of Zucchini's cage.

"Come on, fella," she said, reaching in with her lacquered fingernails.

She grabbed Zucchini at the top of his neck, just behind the ears, and lifted him out of his cage.

"Come on," she said. "I have to take your temperature."

"So!" Dr. Merlin added with purpose. "Pneumonia, eh? What was a little fellow like you doing on Eighty-seventh Street?" He pointed a finger at Zucchini in mock seriousness. "You should know better."

Miss Venucchi set Zucchini down on the metal examining table and momentarily loosened her grip on his neck. With her right hand she adjusted her snap-in hair clip with the velvet bow.

This is it! thought Zucchini.

He summoned all his strength and lunged from the metal examining table. He landed on the floor and sped from the room.

"Wait a minute!" shouted Miss Venucchi, but it was too late. Zucchini was already out on the circular ramp that led down to the main floor of the ASPCA.

"Catch him!" shouted Miss Venucchi.

There was a group of people sitting outside the examining room, each holding some pet, but none of them responded. They all seemed wrapped up in their own thoughts. A large German shepherd broke away from its owner and made a lunge for Zucchini.

"Come back, Moses!" shouted the dog's owner, but Moses paid no mind. He bumped into Miss Venucchi and sent her careening into the banister. Then he snapped viciously at Zucchini's tail.

"Moses!" shouted the dog's owner. He was a tall man without any hair. "Sit, Moses!"

Just then Moses bit Zucchini in the foot. The pain shot through

Zucchini's body. He spun around and dashed back up the ramp on three feet, leaving Moses barking in confusion.

"What was that?" asked a pale lady holding an orange cat.

"Wolves," said the man on her left.

Zucchini turned off the ramp at the third floor and limped down the hallway. His foot throbbed with pain, and he could see that it was bleeding.

I've got to rest, he thought.

He spotted an open door at the end of the hallway and headed through it and into a small office. There was a desk by the wall, and Zucchini hid underneath it, panting heavily. The cut on his foot was deep and he licked it to cleanse the wound and stop the bleeding.

Chapter Eight
Miss Pickett

Miss Pickett had just stepped out for coffee. A coffee wagon came around each morning, and Miss Pickett always made it a point to stop whatever she was doing and get a light coffee and a cinnamon twist. When Zucchini hid under her desk, Miss Pickett was down at the other end of the hall, waiting in line for her treat. She stood next to Mr. Devlin from administration, who inquired about the frogs.

"We haven't received them," said Miss Pickett, eying her cinnamon twist.

"They've been authorized," said Mr. Devlin.

"I know," said Miss Pickett, "but they haven't come."

"I'll look into it," said Mr. Devlin.

Miss Pickett took her snack back to her office and closed the door. She didn't care for Mr. Devlin, and she didn't want him poking his head in, with or without frogs. Mr. Devlin had been hired for what was referred to as his "business head," but he didn't like animals and this annoyed Miss Pickett.

"That for him," she said quietly to herself as she shut the door.

Miss Pickett was a small molelike woman with short brown hair and clear-rimmed glasses that pointed up at the sides. She loved animals and was in charge of the children's zoo at the ASPCA on Ninety-second Street. Children from all over New York, New Jersey, Long Island and parts of Connecticut came to study with her and help care for the animals. Miss Pickett kept over twenty animals in the children's zoo and offered classes twice a week in animal care, handling and history. She took pride in her work and felt it was particularly important in a large city such as New York for children to get to know different kinds of animals. Normally, they would never have the chance.

Miss Pickett took her snack to her desk, pulled out her chair and sat down.

Don't kick me, thought Zucchini, huddling beneath Miss Pickett's desk. He could hear her talking to herself, organizing her thoughts for Tuesday's class.

"Now, let's see," she was saying. Then she dropped her napkin. "Oh, dear," she said. She pushed back her chair, bent down and reached out for her napkin. When she saw Zucchini she gave a little jump. "Oh, my!" she said. She was startled and froze in her position, bent over at the waist, one hand on her desk, the other reaching down toward her napkin.

What will she do with me? thought Zucchini.

"Who are you?" Miss Pickett asked when she had recovered from her shock. She spoke kindly and with great respect, as if she knew Zucchini couldn't answer, but she wanted to ask anyway. "What are you doing down there?" She pushed back her chair and stooped down to get a better look at Zucchini. "Can you be a ferret? That's what you look like. My, my."

Then she noticed the blood. She reached her hand out toward Zucchini, grabbed him gently behind the ears and pulled him toward her. Zucchini felt instantly that she would never hurt him.

"Poor little thing," she said.

"He must be in here."

Miss Venucchi was all excited and stood in the doorway, gasping for breath. Miss Pickett raised a finger to her lips.

"Shh," she said. "Don't frighten him."

"That's him!" said Miss Venucchi. She was pointing at Zucchini. "That's him right there!"

"Shh," repeated Miss Pickett.

"Thank God!" said Miss Venucchi. She collapsed in the chair by the door. "He hasn't had his shots, and we don't want him going around biting anybody."

Not her again, thought Zucchini.

"He's injured," said Miss Pickett. She was stroking Zucchini's fur. "What happened?"

"He got away on me," said Miss Venucchi. She unbuttoned her white lab coat, and Zucchini could see her chest, heaving up and down beneath her tight rayon-and-wool pullover. "He came in with pneumonia a couple of days ago," she continued. "Then he got bit in the foot."

"What happened?" asked Miss Pickett.

"Some police dog bit him on the ramp," said Miss Venucchi. "Should I take him back?"

"No," Miss Pickett said simply. "I'd like to keep him here."

"You want him?" asked Miss Venucchi. She seemed surprised.

"I want him," Miss Pickett replied.

Chapter Nine
Resting Place

Dr. Merlin came up and gave Zucchini his shots and bandaged his foot while Miss Pickett searched for a cage.

"I'm sure I had an extra one," she was saying to herself. "I'm sure of it."

They had moved into the zoo itself, which was located just off Miss Pickett's office. The zoo was a large sunny room with lots of windows. Cages and pens were everywhere. Animals peered at Zucchini from behind glass, mesh and wire, from inside tanks, crates and boxes. A porcupine got up from his nap and stuck out his quills. His name was Louis, and he was three feet long. He pointed his tiny head in Zucchini's direction and stared with frightened eyes.

What a strange thing, thought Zucchini.

Arnold, the crow, was shaking himself. He had been bathing in his water dish, and he shook droplets of water onto his glass window. A white mouse took to her wheel and began treading her way to points unknown; two gerbils looked up from under a mound of wood chips; a raccoon sat up on his hind legs, asking for food; a black snake lifted his head and stuck out his pointy tongue.

"Here it is," said Miss Pickett. She was pulling a metal cage out from behind some packing crates.

Oh, no! thought Zucchini.

"This ought to work," Miss Pickett said. She took a rag from the closet and began dusting the cage. Then she looked for a place to set it up.

"You gonna put him in there?" asked Miss Venucchi. She was holding Zucchini while Dr. Merlin applied the bandage.

"Yes," said Miss Pickett.

"It's so big," said Miss Venucchi. "Put him in something smaller."

"Oh, please, please," said Zucchini. "Someone, help me!"

"I think he'd like the extra room," Miss Pickett suggested. She was setting up the cage between Arnold, the crow, and Louis, the porcupine.

"All righty," Dr. Merlin said cheerfully. "All bandaged up."

"Should I put him in?" asked Miss Venucchi, pointing to the cage.

If she tries, I'll bite her, thought Zucchini.

"I'll do it," Miss Pickett replied.

Dr. Merlin and Miss Venucchi left, and Miss Pickett carried Zucchini toward the cage.

"Here we go," she said.

Arnold, the crow, was peering through his glass with an inquiring gaze as Miss Pickett approached.

"You're quite the little fellow," she said to Zucchini. "I'll just put you in here."

No you won't, thought Zucchini.

Miss Pickett lifted the latch of the cage as Zucchini leaped from her arms and crawled back under her desk. His injured foot throbbed with pain.

I won't go in! he thought. Never! I'd rather die!

"Come on, now," said Miss Pickett. "There's nothing to worry about."

"I think he's scared."

It was a tiny voice, almost too quiet to hear. Zucchini turned his head and there, standing in the doorway, was a boy. He was thin with large eyes and light hair. He wore a white T-shirt and

sneakers, and his loose blue jeans were gathered at the waist by a narrow belt. One of his front teeth was chipped off at the corner.

"Come in," said Miss Pickett.

The boy seemed frightened and didn't move from his place at the door.

"I don't know what we're going to do with this poor ferret," said Miss Pickett. She picked up Zucchini and stroked him gently along the back. "Goodness me."

The boy turned to go.

"You can stay if you like," said Miss Pickett. "Are you visiting?"

"No," said the boy.

"Please, come in. Come in and tell me your name."

The boy hesitated, then moved slowly into the room.

"That's better," said Miss Pickett. "What's your name?"

"Billy," said the boy. His voice was soft.

"How old are you, Billy?"

"Ten," said the boy.

"Do you like animals?"

"Yes," said the boy.

"So do I," said Miss Pickett. "What shall we do with this poor little fellow? Do you have any thoughts?"

"I think he'd like it better in there," said the boy. He pointed to the outgoing-mail bin on Miss Pickett's desk.

He's right, thought Zucchini. I would.

"I think you've got something," said Miss Pickett. "Would you mind moving those letters?"

The boy moved very slowly and cautiously forward and took the letters out of Miss Pickett's mail bin. Then he watched as Miss Pickett set Zucchini down.

"You know a lot about animals, Billy," said Miss Pickett. "I can tell. Thank you for helping me."

"You're welcome," said the boy.

He's nice, thought Zucchini. I wonder why he's so shy.

Chapter Ten
Billy

Billy had always been shy. At least that's the way it had been for as long as he could remember. Sometimes, when he had nothing better to do, he would try and figure out what it was that had started the shyness, or when it was that it started, but he couldn't remember. His teachers at school said it was because Billy's parents were divorced. They had been divorced for two years, and Billy lived with his mother and stepfather. His real father was an actor in Los Angeles, California, and Billy didn't get to see him very much.

"It's hard getting used to a stepfather," Billy's teachers would say. "That's why William is withdrawn."

Billy didn't like being called William, and he didn't think his teachers were right, not completely right anyway. He remembered always liking to be quiet. Even as a tiny boy there was so much to look at and listen to, so much to understand. Too much talking got in the way.

Billy often thought about that and about how things added on to that, how they mounted up. First, there was his father. Billy's father was very outgoing and told jokes really well and always had a quick answer. Billy liked to listen to his father, but he figured he could never be as smart, or as funny, so there wasn't much point in trying. Also, there wasn't any room. In his enthusiasm Billy's father interrupted people a lot.

Then there was Emma. Emma was Billy's five-year-old sister. Everything was easy for Emma, and if she wasn't jabbering away about something you could figure she was asleep. Billy didn't like her jabbering, but sometimes he wished he could be more like her.

Emma doesn't help matters, Billy would think.

It seemed to Billy that his shyness grew as he got older. He thought it had a little bit to do with getting used to a new father, but it was more than that. Maybe it was the sports thing. Billy was never very good in sports, and the older he got, the more that seemed to matter to the other kids. They took sports so seriously, especially the boys. Billy felt left out. He liked swimming, but that was about it. Billy's stepfather liked sports and was always trying to get Billy to play baseball. He was a Phillies fan and kept offering to take Billy to Philadelphia, but Billy never wanted to go.

I guess I'm shy for a lot of reasons, Billy would think, and the more he thought of himself as shy, the worse it got.

Billy's greatest comfort was his love of animals. He understood them in ways he couldn't explain. His feeling for them was something extraordinary. Several times a week he would visit the squirrels in Central Park. He would take them nuts and sit for maybe an hour at a time, not moving a muscle, with five or six or more squirrels surrounding him. There was one squirrel that Billy had gotten to know over a period of several months who would sit up on Billy's shoulder and eat his nuts there.

Billy's stepfather didn't like Billy spending so much time with squirrels. Whenever he heard about it, he seemed to get angry.

"If you're going to the park why don't you play ball, or tag, or some sport?" his stepfather would say. "You're never going to make friends and you don't get enough exercise."

"Don't worry," Billy's mother would say. "Don't force him."

Billy had always wished for a pet of his own. Unfortunately, the rules of his housing development prohibited pets, so he had to be satisfied with the pictures he had cut out of magazines and taped to the walls of his room.

Emma was more interested in trucks. She had her own room, so she couldn't complain about the animal pictures all over Billy's walls, but sometimes she said they were queer.

Billy's housing development was just behind the ASPCA, and Billy would often imagine the different animals he could meet inside the red-brick building. The trouble was, he could never get up the courage to go in.

Someone might yell at me, he would think. They might yell or be cross or ask me what I thought I was doing, or they might talk meanly and say, "What do *you* want?" or "Don't bother me," or something like that.

The day Billy met Zucchini an interesting thing happened. It was Saturday, and he had gotten up early. Everyone else was asleep, so he poured himself some juice, had a bowl of cereal, wrote a short note explaining where he was going and left the house.

First, he walked around for a little while down by the river. He liked to watch the sea gulls and often wished they could tell him about their adventures out over the ocean.

A man came across the footbridge over the highway with two large black dogs off the leash. He wore a sea captain's hat and sat staring at the boats on the river. Billy wondered if the man had once been a sea captain and missed the life at sea, or whether he had never been a sea captain and missed the life at sea. Probably one or the other, Billy figured.

After a while Billy crossed back over the footbridge and headed for the ASPCA. There was a wall sculpture on the side of the building that showed a boy, standing with his arm around a horse's neck, surrounded by animals. The boy looked a lot like Billy, and he liked to pretend it really was him. He was looking at the sculpture when a uniformed attendant called out to him.

"Hey, kid!" shouted the attendant. He was holding an injured pigeon. One of its wings appeared to be broken. "Take this, would ya? I got a' emergency." He pointed to his truck, parked at the curb. "I gotta go."

Billy reached out and took the wounded bird, almost without thinking.

"Just take it in there," said the attendant, pointing toward the ASPCA. "Ask for the clinic." Then he drove off.

Billy glanced down at the pigeon. The bird looked startled and seemed to be waiting for someone to relieve the pain. Billy took a deep breath, turned and headed through the double doors and into the building. Just inside was an information booth.

"Can I help you?" asked the lady in charge. She was perched high on a stool and looked somewhat like a bird herself.

"Where's the clinic?" Billy asked. He hated asking questions and spoke too softly to be heard.

"I can't hear you," said the lady in a loud, raspy voice from up on her stool. "What do you want?"

"The clinic," Billy repeated.

"You'll have to speak up," said the lady. Her eyes were wide, and she blinked like an owl. "Watcha got?"

"A pigeon," said Billy as loudly as he could.

"A pigeon," said the lady. "Is it sick?"

"Hurt," said Billy.

"What?" said the lady. "You'll have to speak up."

"Hurt," said Billy.

"Hurt pigeon," the lady announced. "Emergency. Up the ramp and to your left. Next time ask for the clinic!"

Billy turned and hurried up the ramp. Dr. Merlin and Miss Venucchi were just coming down from upstairs. They had given Zucchini his shots and bandaged his foot and were returning to their work at the clinic.

"Mmm," said Dr. Merlin, spotting the pigeon. "What do we have here?"

"A pigeon," said Billy.

"Oho!" said Dr. Merlin for some reason of his own. "Come in

and set him on the table, son. Set him right down."

"You from upstairs?" asked Miss Venucchi as they moved into the examining room.

"No," said Billy.

"You're not from the children's zoo?"

Billy didn't answer.

"Where ya from?"

"Nowhere," said Billy.

"Oh," said Miss Venucchi, not bothering to ask what he meant by that. "Well, if you like animals you oughta go up. It's on the third floor."

Billy was thinking he'd like to see the children's zoo, but he'd met enough strangers for one day. He had a headache.

"Go on!" Miss Venucchi insisted. She grabbed him by the arm and pulled him toward the door. "There," she said, pointing up the ramp. "It's right up there. Ask for Miss Pickett."

So that was how it happened. Miss Venucchi gave Billy a shove, and he started slowly up the ramp. When he got to the third floor, he turned down the hall, found the children's zoo and stood in Miss Pickett's doorway, afraid to go in.

Chapter Eleven

Mr. Devlin and the Frogs

Five minutes after they put him in the outgoing-mail bin, Zucchini fell asleep. Billy and Miss Pickett stood nearby.

"Would you like to join our class?" Miss Pickett inquired. "We meet on Tuesdays and Thursdays at four. There's no charge."

"I don't know," said Billy.

He wanted to, but he was scared. A whole new group of kids—they'd be friends, he'd be left out. He noticed the clock above Miss Pickett's desk. It said twelve-fifteen. He should be home. They might begin to worry.

"I have to go," he said.

"All right," said Miss Pickett. "I hope we see you on Tuesday."

"Good-bye," said Billy. He took a last long look at Zucchini and left.

When it was time for Miss Pickett to leave, Zucchini was still asleep.

"I guess you were tired," she said. She was bending over the desk, writing a note. "I'm off tomorrow, so I'll see you on Monday. Rest well."

She put a paperweight down on the corner of the note, put on her hat, picked up her purse and left.

Zucchini slept soundly through all of Saturday night and part of Sunday morning. He didn't even hear George, the Sunday Man, when he came in to feed the animals and clean their cages. When George first saw Zucchini sleeping in the outgoing-mail bin he thought he was stuffed.

"Stuffed," George muttered to himself when he first looked down. Then he saw the note.

George,

Please leave ferret in mail bin and do not cage him, as he objects.

Feed one cup grain plus mixed vegetables.

Helen Pickett

When Zucchini woke up, George was gone. He stretched, and rubbed his eyes with his little paws. A pain shot through his back foot, and he turned to discover the bandage. Sunlight streamed through the uncurtained window, landing on the food George had left. Zucchini noticed it, but he had no desire to eat. He was weak, and sick to his stomach as well. Loneliness filled his tiny body. He spent the day looking out the window at the river and the patch of sky between the buildings. He longed to feel strong, longed to find the open prairies. But how could he find them? He didn't even have the strength to think.

Miss Pickett arrived early the next morning.

"Hello," she said warmly, heading for the mail bin. She took off her small navy-blue hat and set it down on the desk along with her keys. "How are you feeling? I thought about you this weekend. Were you lonesome?"

Oh, yes, thought Zucchini. I wish I could tell you.

"They're due at three," said Mr. Devlin. He was leaning into the doorway on his way to somewhere or other. He always appeared to be in transit.

"Excuse me?" said Miss Pickett.

"The frogs," said Mr. Devlin. He was puffing on a cigarette and looked as though he hadn't gotten enough sleep. "The frogs are due at three."

"Fine," said Miss Pickett.

"What's that?" asked Mr. Devlin, pointing at Zucchini.

"A ferret," said Miss Pickett.

"Oh," said Mr. Devlin, not hearing. "What's he doing in there?" He was pointing to the outgoing-mail bin.

"He objects to being caged," answered Miss Pickett.

"The heck with that!" bellowed Mr. Devlin. He dropped some ashes from his cigarette onto the floor. "Put him in a cage!"

Miss Pickett said nothing.

"The heck with that!" repeated Mr. Devlin for reasons of his own. "Sammy'll bring the frogs up at three." Then he left.

"Frogs to you," Miss Pickett mumbled under her breath. She patted Zucchini on top of his head. "Don't listen to him," she said. "He's a dummy." She picked up her hat from the desk and put it on the top shelf of the closet. Then she went into the next room.

Zucchini blinked his tiny eyes in confusion. He tried to stand, but the room began to spin. His head ached, he was sick to his stomach and his foot throbbed with pain. He wondered if he would always feel this way. If that were true, he'd rather die. He lay down and closed his eyes. Nothing mattered.

Chapter Twelve

Decision

On Monday night Billy wouldn't eat his dinner.

"What's up?" his stepfather asked, biting into a crunchy piece of fried chicken.

"Nothing," said Billy.

"There is too," said Emma. "He's lying."

"That's not nice," said Mrs. Ferguson. She was standing behind Emma, filling Emma's glass with milk. In her blue jeans, she looked no more than twenty, hardly old enough to be a mother. "I'll bet Billy's thinking about the ASPCA. Sometimes it's hard to make a decision."

"Not for me," said Emma. She pounded a pat of butter down into her mashed potatoes with a spoon.

"Don't play with your food," said her mother.

"I'm not," said Emma. "I have to mash my butter. It's no good in a disgusting lump."

"Emma, please," said Mr. Ferguson.

"Well, it isn't," said Emma.

"Want to talk about it, Billy?" said Mr. Ferguson. "Maybe I can help."

"I don't know," said Billy. "I want to join, but I wonder what it will be like. Maybe the kids will be mean."

"Why should they be mean?" his mother asked. She had returned to her seat.

"They might be," said Billy.

"Like you," said Emma.

"Emma, please," said Mr. Ferguson. "Why not try it, Billy? That's the way to find out."

The phone rang. It was Billy's father calling from Los Angeles. He asked Billy about school and told him he was acting in a television show called *Beware of the Apes.* He played a mean ape and spent three hours in the makeup room every morning. He said it was hard work. When he asked to speak with Emma she said, "Another time—I have to watch TV." Emma was still mad at her father for leaving and never wanted to talk on the phone.

After dinner, Billy joined Emma by the television set. She was watching a show called *Beat the Clock*, where people did silly things as fast as they could. Emma loved it.

"Look what I can do," she said when the first commercial came on. She sat motionless, clutching a large dump truck and staring at the wall.

"What?" said Billy, not paying attention. He lay stretched out on the couch, thinking about Zucchini. He was hoping they'd left him in the mail bin and not locked him in a cage.

"This," said Emma.

"What," said Billy.

"This."

Billy turned to look at Emma.

"You're not doing anything," he said.

"Yes, I am."

"No, you're not. You're just sitting there."

"Look at my ears," said Emma.

Billy looked at Emma's ears.

"What about them?"

"I'm moving them."

"No, you're not."

"I am. Look."

"I'm looking. You're not moving them."

"I am, you big stupid thing. They're completely moving back and forth."

"No, they're not."

"You're blind," said Emma.

What should I do? thought Billy. I want to go back there so much, but I'm scared. Why? What am I scared of?

"It takes muscles," said Emma. She rammed her dump truck into a nearby chair. "Crash and bash!" she said. "I bet you can't do it."

"Do what?" said Billy.

"Move your ears."

"I don't want to."

"That's not the reason."

"Yes, it is."

"You don't know how," said Emma. "That's the thing."

"Keep quiet for a while," said Billy.

"I'm not teaching you," said Emma.

"Fine," said Billy.

Just then a couple came on *Beat the Clock* and began throwing pies at each other. They wore large rubber boots and witch's hats.

"Are you going out for Halloween?" asked Emma.

"No," said Billy.

"Why not?"

"I'm just not."

"You went out last year."

"Well, I'm not going out this year."

"Is that because you're so old?"

"Maybe," said Billy.

"I know what I'm gonna be. The gigantic chicken monster of outer spaces."

"Outer space," said Billy. "There's only one space and that's everything."

"I know," said Emma.

"Then why did you call it spaces?"

"I made it up, so I can call it what I want. It's up to my decision."

Beat the Clock was ending. The announcer said that everyone should stay tuned for the news.

"I hate news," said Emma.

"Switch the channel," said Billy. He was still stretched out on the couch.

Emma pushed her truck out of the way and got up on her knees. She grabbed the dial and clicked it to CBS. There was a commercial on for McDonald's.

"The beak will be made of cheese," she said.

"What beak?"

"The beak of the great chicken monster. I have it planned. The beak will be completely of old cheese. That way Mama won't mind if I take it. It will be old cheese, and I will carve the beak with a spoon. Into this cheese I'm making a gripping place for my teeth, and then there will be this pointy beak coming out."

"It'll rot," said Billy.

"No, it won't," said Emma.

"It'll rot, and you'll smell. No one will give you any candy."

"They will," said Emma with confidence. "And if I get hungry, I can eat it."

"The candy?" said Billy.

"The beak," said Emma. "I can chew it off from the inside."

"That's the stupidest thing I ever heard," said Billy.

"I'm only five," said Emma.

The McDonald's commercial finished and on came CBS *Newsbreak.*

"Go away," Emma said to the newsman and switched the channel. Carol Burnett was on, wearing a motorcycle jacket and shrieking at a short man in a little girl's jumper.

"O.K.!" said Emma, excitedly. She rocked back off her knees, grabbed her truck and began dumping and loading imaginary stones. Billy closed his eyes and tried to think.

I should go, he thought. I should just go. If it's terrible, I can leave.

"Are you ever going to that animal place?" asked Emma.

It was as if she knew what he was thinking.

"I don't know," said Billy.

"Why are you scared of mean kids? You're so big. You could beat them up, I bet."

"No, I couldn't," said Billy. "You just think I'm big because I'm bigger than you."

"You're very big," said Emma.

"Not really," said Billy.

Sometimes it was nice to have a sister.

Chapter Thirteen

New Name

By Tuesday morning Zucchini felt a lot better. The dizziness was gone and so was the headache. He ate a good breakfast, and the knowledge that he would someday recover filled him with hope. He was still weak, but strength would come. He knew that now. He needed time. He also needed to talk with the other animals.

I need directions, he thought. They might know the way to the open prairies. At least some of them might know. I can't be the only one who's heard of those prairies. Maybe someone will want to go with me. Maybe they belong there too. I have to find my way. This mail bin is better than the rodent house, but it's not my home. Of that I'm sure.

That afternoon Miss Pickett held class. The children were noisy and excited, and all wanted turns holding Zucchini. One girl held him in her arms while another kissed him on the nose. Twin boys grabbed him and pulled in different directions.

I hope I live through this, thought Zucchini. Then he saw Billy. He stood just inside the doorway, not moving, not saying a word.

"Come in, Billy," said Miss Pickett. "I'm glad you're here."

Billy took a deep breath and moved into the room. He smiled nervously.

"Children, this is Billy," said Miss Pickett. "Billy has come to join our class.

Some of the children turned to look at Billy, and a few said hello. Billy smiled another nervous smile, showing the chip in his front tooth.

"Why is his tooth broken?" asked Fred. Fred was eight, wore glasses and always asked a lot of questions.

"I don't know," Miss Pickett responded. "You could ask Billy."

Fred walked over to Billy and looked him in the face. "Why is your tooth broken?" he asked.

"I fell down," said Billy. He was wishing they wouldn't always ask about his tooth.

"On what?" asked Fred. "What kind of hard thing did you fall down on that made it break?"

"Stone steps," said Billy.

"Oh," said Fred, dismissing the whole business. "We don't have stone steps."

"Come in, Billy," said Miss Pickett. "The ferret is doing well."

Billy moved slowly toward the mail bin. He knelt down and looked into Zucchini's eyes.

"Hello," he said.

There was something so understanding in the way he spoke. Zucchini had never known anything like it.

Soon they moved into the next room. Miss Pickett carried the mail bin and set it down on the floor.

Bumpy ride, thought Zucchini as he slid around in the bin.

"Circle around," instructed Miss Pickett. "Pull up your chairs. Quietly, please! Now, does anyone know what we have here?"

"A weasel!" shouted a tall boy at the rear of the class.

"That's close, Charles," said Miss Pickett, holding Zucchini up for everyone to see. "He's in the weasel family, but he has a special name. Does anyone know what it is?"

No one responded, so Miss Pickett called on Billy.

"Billy," she said, "you know. What is our new friend called?"

Billy's throat got suddenly very dry, and he thought he had lost his voice.

"Ferret," he said as best he could.

"Ferret," said Miss Pickett. "That's right. Our new little friend is a ferret, and as you can see, he has hurt his foot."

"What happened to it?" asked Fred.

"He was bitten by a dog," said Miss Pickett.

"We don't have a dog," said Fred.

"That's fine," said Miss Pickett. "Now, he seems to be doing very well. We have disinfected the wound, and also bandaged it as you can see. Boys and girls, this is a black-footed ferret. You'll note his pale yellowish-buff color, his black eye mask, black-tipped tail and, of course, his tiny black feet. This type of ferret is very rare. He's one of our endangered species, and he comes from the prairies of North America."

The prairies! thought Zucchini. She knows!

"Now, this ferret is still a baby. I would say maybe three months old at the most. When he's full grown, he will have a body length of approximately sixteen inches and a six-inch tail."

She knows a lot about me, thought Zucchini.

"Notice, boys and girls, how I'm holding this ferret. I pick him up by bringing my hand up gently but steadily from behind. This way I can hold him by his head and shoulders. Also, as with all animals, and we've talked about this before, boys and girls, my movements are slow. I never move suddenly or the ferret may bite me, and I wouldn't want that."

"Do they have any spit?"

The question came from a dark-haired girl with braids and plump cheeks, sitting up front.

"Repeat your question, Buffy," said Miss Pickett.

"Do they have any spit," said Buffy.

"You mean saliva?" asked Miss Pickett.

"I mean juice in their mouth," said Buffy. "I was wondering because squirrels don't have any spit, and when they get dirty, they sneeze on their paws, and then they clean themselves."

"That's disgusting," said Fred.

"Shut up," said Buffy.

"Buffy, please," said Miss Pickett.

"Well, they do, and I wanna know if ferrets have it like that, or if they're regular."

"I hadn't heard that in respect to squirrels," said Miss Pickett, "but ferrets do have saliva. I don't believe, however, that you should term a condition like that regular or not regular. All creatures have their own special characteristics, including you or me."

"Buffy made that up," said Fred.

"I did not," said Buffy.

"You did too. You are so stupid."

"I am not."

"You are too. You're stupid, and you look like pudding."

"That will do, Fred," said Miss Pickett. "And Buffy, you might like to bring us some research on your theory about squirrels."

"Fat chance," said Fred.

"That will do," said Miss Pickett. "Now, today we're going to name our new friend. Does anyone have any suggestions?"

I have a name, thought Zucchini.

"What would you like to suggest?" Miss Pickett twisted her narrow expandable watchband as she spoke. "We'll take suggestions now, and then we'll have a vote."

"Lenny!" shouted a girl in a red sweater.

"Tipsy!" shouted her friend.

Miss Pickett took the names down on a small pad. "Yes," she said. "Any more?"

Billy had an idea, but he couldn't get himself to raise his hand. He was thinking the other children might laugh. They might think his idea was stupid.

"Trixie!"

"Tuffy!"

"Murphy!"

"Max!"

I hate these names, thought Zucchini.

"Sleepy!"

"Nosy!"

"Sneezy!"

"Zucchini!"

What? thought Zucchini.

"Zucchini," repeated the voice. It was Fred.

That's my name, thought Zucchini.

"Why Zucchini?" asked a boy with braces on his teeth. "That's weird."

"Fred's weird," said Buffy.

"Can you tell us what brought the name to mind, Fred?" Miss Pickett asked.

"I can," said Fred. "There's a ferret at the Bronx Zoo who has that name."

Not anymore, thought Zucchini.

"It means squash," said the girl in the red sweater.

"He looks like a squash," said Fred. "Long and skinny."

The class agreed and gave Zucchini his real name. Zucchini was thinking he was glad they had done the right thing, and Billy was thinking he wished he had had the courage to call out his idea. It had been Zucchini.

Chapter Fourteen

New Creatures

At five o'clock it was time for the children to leave. Billy wanted to stay longer, but he didn't have the courage to ask.

"Would you like to stay awhile?" Miss Pickett inquired. "You can stay until I leave if you'd like."

"O.K.," said Billy.

"Why not show Zucchini around," said Miss Pickett. "Let him meet the other animals."

Yes, please! thought Zucchini. I need my directions!

"Go ahead," Miss Pickett said to Billy. "Pick him up."

Billy was grateful for the chance to hold Zucchini and picked him up gently.

"Here's a hawk," said Billy, holding Zucchini up in front of Trinka's cage.

Trinka was a broad-winged hawk who had flown into a telephone wire and damaged a wing. She would never fly again. When she saw the new visitors she blinked her eyes and backed up slightly.

She looks nice, thought Zucchini. I wish they'd leave us alone so we could talk.

Zucchini saw Arnold, the crow; Louis, the porcupine; and many new creatures. He saw Bimbo and Frances, the turtles whose necks bulged out when they breathed. He saw fifteen shivering baby white mice and two frogs. Ned, the opossum, was eating his fruit; Flora, the rabbit, was cleaning her toes; and a screech owl named Pete had a sign under his window. It had been written by one of the children who had done research on screech owls. It said:

PETE

A SCREECH OWL.

THE TUFTS ON HIS HEAD ARE NOT EARS (ALTHOUGH THEY LOOK LIKE THEM).

THE EARS ARE CONCEALED.

Just then, Mr. Devlin burst in with Sammy and the frogs. Sammy was Mr. Devlin's assistant. He was four feet tall and carried all three crates of frogs with no help from Mr. Devlin.

"I'm sorry they're late," Mr. Devlin called back over his shoulder to Miss Pickett.

She had forgotten all about the frogs, which she didn't want anyway. She already had two frogs, Charlie and Charlie, Jr., and saw no need for any more.

"Put them over there," Mr. Devlin said to Sammy. He pointed to the large table in the corner.

Oh, no! thought Zucchini. Not him! Don't let him put me in a cage! Please!

"There's three dozen," Mr. Devlin said to Miss Pickett, who had just come in.

"Fine," said Miss Pickett.

She had never understood about the frogs. Mr. Devlin had been talking about them for weeks, and Miss Pickett had pretty much ignored the whole thing. She had never thought they'd come.

Billy was standing near the screech owl, holding Zucchini; and after Sammy put the frogs down, Mr. Devlin came over.

"What you got there, son, a squirrel?"

"Ferret," said Billy.

"That's some squirrel," Mr. Devlin said absently. Then he looked back at the frogs. "Have you caged that thing that was in the office?"

"Not yet," Miss Pickett said firmly.

"Well, do it!" said Mr. Devlin, and he turned to leave. "Come on, Sammy."

Sammy was standing over by the frogs, sweating and wiping his forehead with a large handkerchief.

"It's hot," he said. He nodded and smiled several times as he wiped his brow.

"Come on," repeated Mr. Devlin, and they left.

Zucchini watched while Billy helped Miss Pickett set up a tank for the frogs. Then Miss Pickett said it was time to leave.

Don't leave! Please! thought Zucchini. What if that man comes back? He'll put me in a cage, and that will be the end of it. I'll never find my home!

"You can put him in the mail bin, Billy," said Miss Pickett. "It's time to go."

Don't put me in the mail bin, thought Zucchini. Leave me here with the others. I need my directions.

Billy set Zucchini very gently in the mail bin.

"Sorry," he said. Then he reached into his pocket and took out something folded in a napkin. It was a saltine cracker he had saved from lunch. He wanted to give it to Zucchini, but he was afraid to ask. Miss Pickett watched as she put on her hat and collected her keys.

"Would you like to give him the cracker?"

"O.K.," said Billy. He had trouble letting people know when

he was pleased. It always sounded like he didn't care.

"The next class is on Thursday," said Miss Pickett. "Can you come?"

"I think so," said Billy.

"I hope so," said Miss Pickett. "Good-bye."

"Good-bye," said Billy. He gave Zucchini the saltine and left.

What a fine cracker, thought Zucchini. What a nice boy.

Billy wasn't due home for dinner until six-thirty, so he went down to the river. His favorite bench was empty and he sat, watching the boats and the movement of the river.

This might be the best day of my life, he thought. It's almost like I have a pet of my own. He lives just a block away. That's not far.

Billy thought and thought and found himself making all sorts of plans. He would help Zucchini get well, he would make him a nice, soft pillow for his mail bin, and after he got to know Miss Pickett better he'd ask if he could visit every day, maybe twice a day, once before school and once after. He would get a delivery job and save money to buy Zucchini a leash and collar. Then he'd take him for walks around the building. Maybe they would even let him bring Zucchini down by the river. Zucchini would like it there. Billy thought of saving more money and buying a silver tag that said ZUCCHINI on it, maybe even ZUCCHINI, *I belong to Billy Ferguson,* if they would let him.

Chapter Fifteen

Caring

That night Billy talked all the way through dinner about his most wonderful afternoon and the adorable ferret who was sick and injured, but was getting well. Emma was amazed.

"First, you don't talk hardly for a minute, and then we sit down for this dinner, and you completely talk all the way through," she said.

"Let Billy finish," said her mother. "Don't interrupt."

"I'm not," said Emma. "Sarah stole all the Play-Doh at school today. She hid it in her underpants."

"Please," said Mr. Ferguson. "We'll hear about that when Billy's through."

"I have to wait 'til Thursday," said Billy. "That's when the next class is. I hope they take good care of him."

"Maybe you could go tomorrow," suggested his mother. She wore her blue jeans as usual and a loose peasant blouse with small flowers on it. She pushed a strand of her straight brown hair back behind her left ear. "Tomorrow's a school holiday, remember. You could call and ask."

"No," said Billy. "They probably wouldn't let me."

"No harm in asking," his mother said. "Excuse me." She got

up to clean some green paint off her thumb. She was a painter and had been working in her studio all afternoon.

"No harm in asking," repeated Mr. Ferguson. He helped himself to some salad. "You have to ask for what you want."

"Can I have a Halloween party?" said Emma.

"Not now, Emma," said Mr. Ferguson. "We're talking to Billy."

"No harm in asking," said Emma.

"When we're finished with Billy. You see, Bill, you have to ask. I just asked for more money at work, and I'm getting it. There's even talk of my opening up a new branch."

"Of a tree?" asked Emma.

"No," said Mr. Ferguson. "Not a tree branch. A branch of a store."

"I never heard of a store with branches," said Emma. "It must look funny."

"Different kind of branches," said Billy. "It's not what you think."

Mrs. Ferguson sneezed.

"God bless you," said her husband.

"Don't open your eyes," said Emma.

"Excuse me?" said her mother.

"Don't open your eyes," said Emma. "If you open your eyes when you sneeze, your eyes pop out."

"I don't think so, dear," said Mr. Ferguson.

"Oh, yes," said Emma. "Tracy said. If you open your eyes when you sneeze, they're gonna pop right out, so you better not do it."

"I'm sure that's not true," said Mrs. Ferguson, blowing her nose on her napkin.

"Well, nobody better try it," said Emma. "I don't want a mother and a daddy and a brother who don't have any eyes. Shut 'em up tight."

"Don't worry about it," said Mr. Ferguson.

"But can I have a Halloween party?" Emma asked.

"I don't see why not," said Mrs. Ferguson.

"Great," said Emma. "And I'm telling Ronald he can't be the great chicken monster. He wants to, but he's out of luck 'cause that's what I'm gonna be, and you can't have two."

"I guess not," said Mr. Ferguson.

"Sam is maybe going to put makeup on him instead."

"That'll be nice," said Mrs. Ferguson.

"No it won't," said Emma. "He'll have big scars and blood coming out. It'll be gross."

That night Emma knocked on Billy's door.

"Can I come in a minute?" she asked.

"O.K.," said Billy. He was looking through his collection of *National Geographic* magazines for a picture of a ferret. If he found one he planned to write ZUCCHINI underneath it and put it up on his wall.

"What I want to know is," said Emma, as she sat down on the end of the bed, "will you take me to that animal place?"

"I'll see," said Billy.

"Why won't you?"

"I said I'll see. I didn't say I wouldn't, I said I'll see."

"Does that mean maybe?"

"Yes."

"Does that mean you'll think about it?"

"Yes."

"When will you think about it?"

"Later."

"Why won't you think about it now?"

"Because I'm busy now. I'll think about it later."

Emma looked at the bedspread. She was about to cry.

"You wanna help me look for a picture of a ferret?" Billy asked.

"O.K.," said Emma. She rubbed her eyes.

"Here. You look through this magazine."

"O.K. What does exactly a ferret look like?"

"It's long and skinny," said Billy. "It's like a squirrel that's long and skinny and very beautiful."

Chapter Sixteen

Friends

At seven-thirty the next morning, Zucchini woke up with a start. He heard the sound of a key turning in the lock of the front door of the office. The door swung open and in came Priscilla. Priscilla had come to clean the office. She was stout and carried a pail.

"I think I'll start in here," said Priscilla, setting down her pail.

Start what? thought Zucchini.

Priscilla went over to the broom closet and got out her mops and rags and brooms and began working and singing.

"Home, home on the range," sang Priscilla, "where the deer and the antelope play. . . ."

She had started dusting over by the window and hadn't noticed Zucchini.

"Open up this window," she said to herself. "Get me some air."

With that, she pulled up the window and went on with her song.

Zucchini's first impulse was to run, head through the open window, find a ledge maybe and work his way down the outside of the building. It would work if only he had the strength. But no. He was still weak. He'd have to wait.

"Where seldom is heard a discouraging word . . ." sang Priscilla.

Then Zucchini noticed the door. Priscilla had left it ajar.

I could get out and look around, he thought. I'm weak and I don't have directions, but at least I can search for escape routes. I'm strong enough for that. I'll creep out, have a look around and be back before Miss Pickett comes in.

He climbed out of the mail bin, and crouching low, so as not to alarm Priscilla, he jumped down off the desk. A pain shot through his injured foot, but he kept on. Silently, he crept out into the hallway and looked in both directions. To the left he noticed the ramp leading down to the clinic. His foot throbbed with pain as he headed down the ramp, past the clinic where he could hear dogs barking furiously from inside.

There's trouble, he thought.

He stopped and peered down the ramp to the main floor. The information lady was perched high on her stool, but otherwise the lobby was empty. He continued down the ramp, and when he reached the bottom, he turned and headed for the back of the building. Just then Mr. Devlin stepped out of the elevator.

Zucchini stopped dead in his tracks. He wanted to run, to get as far away as possible, but he couldn't move. He was paralyzed with fear. He stood, frozen like a statue, and peered at Mr. Devlin with bulging eyes.

Billy woke up at eight. Emma was pounding on his door, calling him names.

"Wake up, you big nu-nu," she said. "You'll miss the whole day."

"I'm awake," said Billy. He turned over and pulled the covers up over his head. "And don't call me names. It isn't nice."

"Can't you pull a joke?" asked Emma.

"Take a joke," said Billy.

"What?" said Emma.

"Take a joke. You don't pull a joke. You take a joke."

"What?" said Emma.

"Never mind," said Billy.

"Do you want French toast, or an omelet?"

"Nothing."

"Nothing?"

"There's no school today. Why did you wake me up?"

"Mom said. Do you want French toast, or an omelet?"

"Nothing. I want to sleep."

Mrs. Ferguson hurried into the room. She wore a T-shirt with STP OIL TREATMENT written on the front.

"Time to get up," she said. "I have to take some drawings in this morning, and I need you up and organized."

"I'm going with Mom," said Emma. "It's supertendon's conference day."

"Superintendent's," said Billy.

"I know," said Emma. "I can say it how I want, but there's no school, so I'm going with Mom. She can't take us both, because one child is enough."

"I don't want to go," said Billy.

"Will you go to the ASPCA?" asked his mother. She was opening the venetian blinds.

"No," said Billy.

"Why not?"

"There's no class . . ."

"They may let you go anyway," said his mother. "Why don't you call and ask?"

"No," said Billy.

"Why don't you wanna ask?" said Emma. She had picked up one of Billy's horse statues and was walking it along the border of the rug.

"Never mind," said Billy.

After breakfast, Billy went out. He crossed the small courtyard in front of his building, aimlessly kicking at stones and small bits of garbage.

Why can't I ask for anything? he thought. It's so stupid. All they can say is no.

He got up to the front door of the ASPCA and stopped. He stared through the glass into the lobby.

I'll go tomorrow, he thought. No big deal.

He turned and walked toward the footbridge over the busy FDR Drive. As he started up the stairs, he noticed something moving toward the highway. It was an animal, small and in a great hurry. In a flash, Billy recognized Zucchini.

"NO!" he screamed, but Zucchini kept on. He was heading straight for the traffic, cars zooming by at sixty miles an hour.

"ZUCCHINI!" screamed Billy. "STOP!"

He wanted to close his eyes, not to see the terrible accident, but his eyes wouldn't close. He just stood and screamed, and Zucchini heard the screams. He veered sharply to the right and ran headlong into a garbage can. Stunned, he lay motionless by the side of the highway.

Billy ran as fast as he could. When he reached Zucchini, he bent down.

"Are you all right?" he said softly.

Zucchini opened his eyes. He looked into Billy's face.

"You're alive," said Billy.

Zucchini lay very still, looking at Billy. He couldn't remember what had happened. He only knew he was looking into the kindest face he had ever seen.

"You have to be careful," said Billy. "You can't go running toward cars. You could get killed."

Thoughts came tumbling back into Zucchini's tiny brain. He remembered running from Mr. Devlin by the elevator, escaping from the building, fearing for his life, not looking where he was going.

"You gotta look," said Billy. "You have to."

Very slowly he picked up Zucchini and sat down, cross-legged, on the sidewalk. He held Zucchini on his lap, and they rested that way for several minutes.

"Let's go by the river," said Billy after a while. "There's grass there and tiny trees and birds. It's a good place."

Billy got up and carried Zucchini very carefully toward the footbridge. Zucchini let himself relax. He felt weak, but secure, more secure than he had felt in his whole life, except very early maybe, with his mother.

Chapter Seventeen

Hot Dogs and Sauerkraut

When they got across the bridge, Billy carried Zucchini to the grass and sat down. The view was beautiful, a great expanse of blue sky with smokestacks forming patterns in front. The river rushed by carrying tugs and barges, all sorts of boats. Gulls flew overhead. The sun was bright, the breeze was soft and cool, but not cold, just nice. They stayed there in silence for a long time, Billy stroking Zucchini gently, and Zucchini relaxing and looking about. Then a hot dog man came by.

"I'm gonna buy us a hot dog," said Billy. "I've got lunch money."

He got up and carried Zucchini toward the hot dog wagon. Zucchini could smell the hot dogs and the sauerkraut cooking.

"Whaddaya want?" asked the hot dog man when they reached the side of the wagon.

"Hot dog," said Billy.

"Whaddaya want on?" said the man. He wore an engineer's cap and a scarf around his neck. He breathed heavily.

"Mustard and sauerkraut, please," said Billy.

The man picked up a hot dog roll and threw back one of the metal doors covering the food bins on his wagon. With a pair of tongs, he pulled out a hot dog and put it on the roll. Then he slammed shut the metal door, opened the one next to it, pulled out a helping of sauerkraut, slammed shut the door and loaded the sauerkraut onto the hot dog. Then he scooped some mustard out from a smaller metal bin with a spoon and put that on top of the sauerkraut.

"This for da squirrel?" he said.

"Ferret," said Billy, but the man didn't hear.

Billy paid the hot dog man, took the hot dog and moved back to the grass.

"Try this," he said. He held a piece of sauerkraut up in front of Zucchini's nose.

Zucchini snapped at the sauerkraut with his tiny teeth, chewed it and swallowed it down. It was delicious. Then he had half the hot dog.

What a meal, he thought. The best I ever had.

After lunch, they had a short nap. Lying on the grass in the sunlight with Billy's arm around him, Zucchini wished he could stay just that way forever. Then Billy suggested a walk.

"I'll show you the river," he said.

Zucchini had never seen more than a bit of the river, never seen grass, never seen more than a patch of sky. He had never seen boats, or bridges, or sea gulls or clouds, really. Billy stopped at Seventy-third Street, and they watched a tiny tugboat pull a huge barge loaded with cement.

Tough little boat, thought Zucchini.

"I should take you back," Billy said at last. "I have to go home, and I can't take you. They don't allow pets in my building."

Back! thought Zucchini. Not back!

"I know you don't want to go," said Billy, "but at least they'll take care of you. I can't leave you on the street. I'll come and see you every day, I promise."

So back they went, Billy walking the twenty blocks without a rest. He had put off returning, and now it was after four. His mother would be worried.

When they reached the children's zoo, Miss Pickett was on the phone.

"I don't care about that," she was saying. "I want him back."

She looked up and burst into a big smile. "Zucchini!" she said. "You found him!"

Billy moved slowly into the office.

"Where was he?" asked Miss Pickett.

"By the highway," said Billy.

"Oh, my," said Miss Pickett. She reached out and took Zucchini from Billy.

Zucchini's heart sank.

"Come here, my little one," said Miss Pickett. She held Zucchini and patted him on the head. "Thank you, Billy. Thank you for finding him."

"That's O.K.," said Billy. "I'd better go now."

Come back soon, thought Zucchini. Please come back.

When Billy had gone, Miss Pickett put Zucchini into his mail bin, gave him a fresh bowl of water and sat at her desk to finish up some paperwork.

Zucchini had some thinking to do. He was exhausted from his day out, his foot still hurt, and he was sore from having smashed into the garbage can. His headache was severe, but still, he had to think. Billy filled his mind and heart. How could he leave him? He had a friend, someone who loved him, someone who cared, someone who fed him sauerkraut and promised to visit every day. What would he find in the prairies that he didn't already have? More space? Maybe, but what would he do in it? He couldn't answer that.

Miss Pickett put away her papers and looked at Zucchini.

"It's time for me to leave," she said. Then she picked up the mail bin and carried Zucchini into the zoo. "You'll sleep in here tonight," she said. "You're better off."

She set down the mail bin, left the zoo, locked the door and put the key in her purse.

"No trips tonight," she said to herself. Then she left.

Chapter Eighteen

Arnold

Zucchini sat up on his hind legs and peered out nervously from inside his mail bin. He was surrounded by animals: Jackson, the snake; Arnold, the crow; Flora, the rabbit, and all the rest. They stared with suspicion at this new intruder with the bandaged foot, each one on guard, prepared, ready for trouble.

"Hello, everybody," said Zucchini.

No one responded.

"I'm Zucchini."

Still nothing.

"I'm happy to be here. I've been wanting to talk to you."

"What are we to think?" said Flora. She sat on a large leaf of limp lettuce, twitching her rabbit nose.

"About what?" said Zucchini.

"About you," said Flora.

"What about me?" said Zucchini.

"Are you friendly? What do you want? Why are you here? What's that thing on your foot? How long are you staying? Do we have to share our food? Things like that."

"Oh, I'm friendly," said Zucchini. "You can be sure of that. I was worried about whether you were friendly. There's an awful lot of you. If you weren't friendly, I'd be in real trouble."

"We're friendly," said Jackson. He was all wound around his fake tree, flicking his forked tongue. "That's the way we are. We're fair, if you're fair."

"I'm glad to hear that," said Zucchini.

"But we don't think you're fair," said the snake.

"Oh, I'm fair," said Zucchini.

"We don't think so," said the snake.

"Why not?" said Zucchini.

"We're locked in cages, and you roam around wherever you please. You call that fair?"

"I don't," said Ned, the opossum. He was eating a grape and stared at Zucchini with piercing eyes set high in his narrow head.

"Oh, please," said Zucchini. "Don't be mad. It wasn't my idea to be in this mail bin. And anyway, I'm not lucky. I have pneumonia, someone bit me in the foot, and I'm trapped here when I have to get home. I'm not lucky at all."

"Better luck next time," said the snake.

Why are they ganging up on me? thought Zucchini. I mean no harm. I'd better do something to show them I'm friendly.

"Listen," he said. "I can open your cages. We can all be out together."

"We-don't-want-any-favors-from-you-you-think-you're-so-smart-well-we-don't," said Flora very fast and unfriendly-like.

"I'm not smart," said Zucchini. "I'm tiny and young and very inexperienced."

"Forget it," said Jackson. "Forget the whole thing."

"Psst!"

It was Arnold, the crow. "Can you come here for a minute?" he asked.

I'm glad someone's friendly, thought Zucchini.

"I wonder if you would do me a favor," said the crow.

"Sure," said Zucchini.

"Could you open the back door of my cage? We could talk better that way."

Zucchini went behind Arnold's cage and opened the latch.

"Thanks," said Arnold. "And don't worry about the others. They'll warm up. They always do."

"I'm relieved to hear that," said Zucchini.

"Listen," said the crow. "I've got to get out of here."

"Me too," said Zucchini. "I've been wanting to talk to someone. I need directions."

"I know a way out if you'll help me," said Arnold. "There's a lady who comes around here sometimes to clean."

"Priscilla," said Zucchini.

"I don't know her by name," said the crow, "but every time she comes, she opens the window. Now, she comes early, always before Miss Pickett. If you could open my cage the next time she opens the window, I could fly out. I think I can still fly."

"Sure," said Zucchini. "Maybe I'll go with you."

"Can you fly?"

"No, but I can climb. I could climb down."

"I'm sorry to bother you with this," said the crow, "but it's very important. I have to get to Staten Island. They're expecting me."

"No trouble," said Zucchini.

"I'm much obliged," said the crow.

Zucchini wondered who was expecting Arnold on Staten Island, but he didn't want to pry. "It's nice to have someone to talk to," he said. "Everyone else is so unfriendly."

"I'm not unfriendly," said a white mouse whose cage was in the corner. "I was just asleep."

"Hello, mouse," said Zucchini. "Want me to let you out?"

"No thanks," said the mouse. "I have my wheel."

Zucchini didn't understand that, but he let it pass. He turned to the crow. "Could I ask you something?"

"Feel free," said the crow.

"I'm looking for my home," said Zucchini. "I see it sometimes when I'm asleep. It's an open place with lots of light and air and different smells and beautiful colors. It's in the prairies near a place called Oklahoma. At least that's what I've heard. Do you know where that is?"

"It's far from here," said the crow. "That much I know."

"Where's here?"

"New York City. The prairies are a distance off."

"I see."

"I tell you what," said the crow. "Ask Treffinger."

"Who's Treffinger?"

"That prairie vole in the corner. He'd know if anybody would."

Zucchini turned to regard Treffinger. The vole was small, but stocky, with sharp, beady eyes, a short furred tail and invisible ears. He sat up on his hind legs, his front paws deftly shelling a sunflower seed.

"West," said Treffinger. He popped the seed into his mouth and chewed rapidly. His tiny cheeks were puffed to twice their size.

"Thank you," said Zucchini. He paused a moment, then continued. "Where's west?"

"Consider the sun," said Treffinger.

"In what way?" said Zucchini.

"The sun sets in the west," said Treffinger. "Head straight for the setting sun, and you'll have it."

"Thank you," said Zucchini.

"Of course there's your other option," continued the vole.

"What's that?" Zucchini moved closer to Treffinger's cage.

"Leave in the morning." Treffinger uncovered another seed from beneath his tumble of wood shavings. "If you leave in the morning just spot the rising sun."

"Then what?"

"Spot the rising sun and head the other way. That'll be west too."

"Thank you," said Zucchini. "Have you been there?"

"Not me."

"Oh," said Zucchini. "With a name like yours, I thought you might have."

"Treffinger?" said Treffinger.

"Treffinger what?" said Zucchini.

"That's my name," said Treffinger.

"I know," said Zucchini, "but why do you mention it?"

"You said my name made you think I'd been to the prairies."

"Oh, not Treffinger," said Zucchini. "It was the prairie vole part that got me thinking."

"I see," said Treffinger. "Well, no, I haven't. I've heard good things about it, though."

"Want to come with me?" asked Zucchini.

"No," said the vole. "I'd have to set up a whole new life. I'm organized here."

"There's more to life than being organized," said Zucchini. "At least it seems that way to me."

"You could be right," said Treffinger, "but there's no way of knowing."

"I suppose not," said Zucchini.

"It's good enough for me right here," said Treffinger. He was shoving his wood shavings into a large mound at the rear corner of his cage. "I'm easy to please."

"Well, thanks again," said Zucchini, and he turned back to the crow.

Arnold had moved out of his cage and was sitting on the Formica counter top, watching the patterns of the late afternoon sun as it streaked in through the window.

"Could I ask another thing?" said Zucchini.

"Feel free," said the crow.

"I want to find my home."

"Yes," said the crow.

"That's all I've cared about for almost as long as I can remember."

"Yes," said the crow.

"First, this groundhog told me there was no other place, only the rodent house. That didn't seem right."

"It wasn't."

"I know. Well, I didn't listen to him, and I left. Now, I'm

trapped here, and I still want to find where I belong. I want that very much, but I met a boy. He's very nice. He put me in my mail bin. He took me to the river. He gave me hot dogs and sauerkraut. He visits me. He cares for me. He gives me crackers. He really is my friend."

"That's wonderful."

"I know," said Zucchini, "but should I leave him? That's what I don't know. Maybe I'll never find my home. I could never find it, and while I'm out looking, I could lose the boy."

"You can't be sure of boys," said the crow. "They grow up. They change."

"Not this one," said Zucchini. "He's special."

"That may be," said the crow. "Only you can decide."

"I guess you're right," said Zucchini. "Thanks for listening."

"My pleasure," said the crow. "Thanks for agreeing to help me get out of here."

"No problem," said Zucchini.

"Don't forget," said the crow.

"I won't," said Zucchini. "I promise."

Chapter Nineteen

One-Day Service

When Billy arrived home, he was greeted by a loud crashing noise. It was Emma's rock tumbler. Her aunt had given it to her so she could shine rocks and make jewelry, and her stepfather had helped her set it up the night before. They had put it in the rear bathroom, but the noise of tumbling rocks filled the apartment.

"Is that you, Billy?" Mrs. Ferguson was in the kitchen hurrying to get the dinner ready.

"It's me," said Billy. He set his schoolbooks down on the hall table and went into the kitchen. "How long do we have to listen to those rocks?"

"Three weeks," said Mrs. Ferguson.

"Three weeks?" said Billy.

"I'm afraid so," said Mrs. Ferguson. She moved to the stove, grabbed the cover of a large pot with a plaid pot holder and dropped in four ears of corn.

"It sounds awful," said Billy.

"I know."

"It sounds like it's grinding something, like the gears are broken."

"Daddy says it's a little bit broken, but not to worry about it."

"I hope it doesn't come apart and spin the rocks and sand and water all over the bathroom."

"Me too," said Mrs. Ferguson. "Wash up and help me set the table."

Billy went to the sink and washed his hands.

"Why are you all dressed up?" he asked.

"I'm not," said his mother. "Just my slacks. I had an appointment at Harper and Row."

"I can't believe it's supposed to spin like that for three weeks," said Billy.

"Neither can I," said his mother.

Billy collected the silverware from the drawer and brought it into the dining alcove.

"What did you do today?" his mother asked.

"I was with the ferret," said Billy. "It was so wonderful. I showed him the river."

"You went to the ASPCA?"

"I was walking by there, and I saw him. He almost got hit by a car."

"Oh, no," said Mrs. Ferguson. "What was he doing outside?"

"I don't know," said Billy. "We had a great time. I was with him all day."

Billy came back into the kitchen to get the napkins and glasses and Emma's plastic Flintstones mug.

"I wish I could keep him here," he said. "He doesn't like the ASPCA."

"He probably likes it fine." Mrs. Ferguson had that tone in her voice that made it sound as if she didn't really believe what she was saying, and she mainly wanted to change the subject.

"He doesn't like it," said Billy. He set down the glasses and the mug and came back for Emma's twisted see-through straw. "Why can't we have pets?" he asked.

"You know why. The apartment doesn't allow it."

"Why don't they allow it?"

"Some don't, that's all."

"That's not a good reason."

"It's just the rules."

"Who makes the rules?"

"I'm not sure." Mrs. Ferguson moved to the sink and began washing lettuce.

"Couldn't we find out and get them changed? I bet there's a lot of people in this building who'd like to have pets."

"It wouldn't work," said his mother.

"Why not?"

"They don't change rules like that." His mother sounded vague.

"How do you know?"

"Please, Billy, I need to concentrate on this dinner, or I'll never get it ready. Slice the radishes."

Billy went to the drawer and took out a sharp knife. Just then the front door opened.

"Look! Look! Look!"

It was Emma, calling from the front hall.

"We're in the kitchen," called her mother.

"Come on, you *people*!"

"We're in the kitchen," repeated Mrs. Ferguson. "You come here."

"Here I come!" shouted Emma. She ran into the kitchen, carrying a cardboard box. "Look at this!" She held out the box. It was a dime-store box with a clear plastic window that used to hold a Bat Man Halloween costume.

"Explain the whole thing, Emma," said Mr. Ferguson. He followed her into the kitchen, taking off his tan crew-neck pullover on the way.

"It's mine," said Emma, holding out the box.

Billy peered through the plastic window. Inside was a baby white mouse.

"Isn't that the smallest thing that could be?" said Emma. She reached for the cover. "Here goes."

"Not in the kitchen," said Mrs. Ferguson.

"I can manage," said Emma.

"Not in the kitchen!"

Billy was stunned. How could it be? How could she have a pet when he was just told he couldn't have one?

Mrs. Ferguson turned off the corn, and they went into the living room. Billy hung back in the doorway, confused, jealous, fighting tears.

"Talk about small, and you'll be talking about this mouse," said Emma.

"Come on in, Bill," said Mr. Ferguson. "Emma, explain the whole story."

Billy didn't move.

"The whole story is, this is my mouse."

"We can't have pets here," said Mrs. Ferguson.

"She knows," said Mr. Ferguson.

"I know," said Emma, "but it's very small. You could hide it in a minute."

"We're not going to be hiding any mice," said her mother. "What's the whole story?"

Emma pulled off the cover. The mouse sat shivering in the corner of the box.

"Hello, you teeniest, tiniest, weeniest thing."

"Don't let it out," said Mrs. Ferguson.

"I won't," said Emma.

"Emma was given the mouse at Tracy's," said Mr. Ferguson.

"Myra from upstairs gave it to me," said Emma.

"When I went to pick her up, there it was," continued Mr. Ferguson. "It's going back later tonight. The Terrymans agreed to keep it there."

"But it's mine," said Emma. "That's the big thing."

It's not fair, thought Billy. He bit his lower lip to keep from crying.

Mr. Ferguson turned to his wife.

"It looks like it's going through," he said. He was talking about his job transfer.

"That's wonderful!" said Mrs. Ferguson. She'd been hoping for the move. Fresh air to breathe, beautiful landscapes to paint, an answer to her prayers.

"We might be moving to the country, kids," said Mr. Ferguson. "What do you think about that?"

Billy's stomach went into a knot.

"We'll know Monday," continued Mr. Ferguson. He turned to his wife. "It seems that audio equipment is booming these days. Everyone wants the best in sound."

"I don't," said Emma.

Billy felt suddenly numb. The idea of moving was too much, a whole new school, hundreds of children he'd never seen before, new teachers, new neighbors and worst of all, he'd have to leave Zucchini. It was a nightmare.

"Wanna know his name?" said Emma.

"Sure," said Mrs. Ferguson. "Then let's eat. Everything's overdone."

"One-Day Service," said Emma.

"That's an unusual choice," said her mother.

"See, Tracy and I were playing on the front steps, jumping off like circus men, and Myra came with her mouse that had three babies. This is one of the very babies." Emma reached out and grabbed for the mouse who darted to the other corner of the box.

"Don't grab it," said Billy.

"It's my mouse," said Emma. "Myra said I could have it, and I said great, and then I said in my mind, 'What will be the name of this very tiny mouse?' and I decided to close my eyes and open them like this"—Emma closed her eyes tightly, then popped them open—"and the first name I saw was the sign across the street, and I asked Myra what it said. She's nine, and she can read really good, and she said 'One-Day Service,' so that's the name of this very tiny mouse. Hello, One-Day Service."

"That's quite a name," said Mr. Ferguson.

"You bet," said Emma. "See, there's a dry cleaners over there."

"Why didn't you name it Dry Cleaners?" asked Billy.

" 'Cause it wasn't the first sign," said Emma. "It had to be. I decided in my mind. Look at the toes. You can't hardly even almost see them. You need a telescope."

Normally, Billy would have corrected her. "Microscope," he would have said, but tonight was different. He went down the hall and shut himself in the bathroom with the rock tumbler and cried.

Chapter Twenty

Memo From the Frog Man

INTER-OFFICE MEMO

FROM THE DESK OF STUART DEVLIN

It has come to my attention of late that certain unauthorized animals have been roaming the premises in various and sundry areas at various and sundry times. THIS WILL STOP.

S.D.

INTER-OFFICE MEMO page 2

Post the enclosed.

ANIMAL RULES

1. NO UNAUTHORIZED BEHAVIOR.
2. EVERY ANIMAL TO HIS OWN CAGE.
3. NO WALKING AROUND THE BUILDING.

"Oh, dear," Miss Pickett sighed when she had finished reading the memo. She had just arrived for work and hadn't yet removed her hat. She got up, went into the zoo and set up a cage.

Zucchini was still asleep. He was so exhausted that he didn't wake up as Miss Pickett lifted him out of his mail bin, carried him to the cage and put him inside. He still didn't have his full strength, and his day by the river and his near disaster by the highway had tired him. Also, he had been up late with the other animals, and tired as he had been, the excitement had made it hard for him to sleep. His bandage had begun to itch, and he had spent over an hour chewing on it until he had gotten it off. He felt better after that, but still it was a long time before he fell asleep. Once he did fall asleep, he heard nothing until Miss Pickett slammed shut the door of his cage.

"You've taken off your bandage," Miss Pickett was saying. "And, dear me, it's lucky you were asleep. I never would have gotten you in."

In where? thought Zucchini. He pulled himself through the haze into wakefulness. Where am I?

When he saw the wire mesh in front of his eyes, he was filled with panic. Oh, no! he thought. Not another cage! What will become of me?

"I'll tell you a secret," said Miss Pickett. She bent down closer to the cage and began whispering. "We'll only keep your cage locked during the day, when *he's* around. Before I leave at night, I'm going to unlock it. You'll have the run of the zoo." She stood up straight again and looked down at Zucchini with a pitying expression. "The poor little fellow," she said. "He doesn't understand."

Billy was early for class. When he reached Miss Pickett's office, he was surprised not to see Zucchini in the mail bin. Miss Pickett was stacking some books in the corner and looked up as Billy came in.

"Don't be concerned," she said. "He's in the zoo. We had to cage him. Mr. Devlin was causing trouble."

Billy said nothing. He went straight into the zoo and found the cage with his ferret curled up in the corner.

"Hello," said Billy.

Zucchini opened his eyes. His friend had come. He stretched and moved to the front of the cage. Billy put his finger through the wire mesh and scratched Zucchini along the bridge of his nose.

"You may remove him from the cage," said Miss Pickett. "It's almost time for class."

Billy opened the cage and took Zucchini out. He carried him to the window.

"There's the river," he said. "You can see a small part of it through the window. That's where we were."

I wish we were there now, thought Zucchini.

When it was time for class, Miss Pickett asked Billy to put Zucchini in the mail bin. Zucchini was glad to be out of the cage and sat watching as the children gathered their chairs around.

"I have an announcement to make," said Miss Pickett. "Let's all get settled as quickly as possible. Fred, spit out your gum. Fiona, put away your monster."

"It's not a monster," said Fiona. "It's an ape doll."

"Whatever it is, this is not the time for it," said Miss Pickett. "Settle down, please."

When it was quiet, Miss Pickett continued.

"Children, I have something very nice to announce. One week from Saturday we will have Parents' Day. All the parents will be invited. We will show them our zoo and our animals, and we will tell them about the things we do here. We will have punch and cookies . . ."

"I don't like punch," said Fred.

"All right," said Miss Pickett. "We will have punch and cookies, and Fred can have water."

"I don't want water," said Fred.

"Please," said Miss Pickett.

"If there's juice, I'll have that," said Fred. "I like certain kinds of juices."

"Fred, please," said Miss Pickett. Then she continued. "I think the very best part of Parents' Day will be this. You will each choose an animal to give a report on. This will be an oral report. Does anyone know what an oral report is?"

"It's like a thermometer," said Fiona. "It goes in your mouth."

"That's close," said Miss Pickett. "Oral does have to do with your mouth. An oral report is a report that you give by talking, not by writing. You will each give a short talk on the animal of your choice. Today, we will choose our animals. Who has a special request? Please, raise your hands."

Of course, Billy wanted Zucchini. But an oral report, a speech in front of people, parents! Not that. He couldn't do it. He'd be shy. Make a mistake. He'd say something stupid, and they'd laugh, or he'd forget what to say, and they'd be mean. What's that jerk doing up there? they'd think.

Billy will pick me, thought Zucchini.

"I want Flora," said Fred. "I know about rabbits."

"I want Trinka," said Fiona.

"Children, please!" said Miss Pickett. "How many want Flora? Raise your hands."

"I do," said Fred.

"Me too," said Buffy. She sat by the window eating a large chocolate cupcake.

"Buffy has a cupcake," said Fred.

"Fred, please," said Miss Pickett.

"My mother made it, and I'm gonna eat it," said Buffy, licking the chocolate icing with her tongue. She had chocolate on her chin, her fingers, her nose and her left ear.

"Fine," said Miss Pickett. "Get a paper towel from the rack."

Buffy stuffed the remains of the cupcake into her mouth and went to get a paper towel.

"You should limit yourself to organic treats," said Fred.

"I don't hear you," said Buffy.

"You'll get fat and your teeth will disintergrate."

"Like your brain."

"That will do," said Miss Pickett. "Let's continue. Are there any more requests for Flora?"

"Me," said Buffy.

"I already have your name," said Miss Pickett. "I'm marking

you all down, and then I'll make the decision after I've heard from everyone. Any more for Trinka?"

"Me," said Fiona. "I already said."

"All right," said Miss Pickett. "Zucchini?"

Billy was slouched down in his chair, staring at his belt.

I guess he's not listening, thought Zucchini.

"Billy," said Miss Pickett. "You want Zucchini, don't you?"

"No," said Billy.

The word shot through Zucchini like a knife.

"Excuse me?" said Miss Pickett. She had already written Billy's name down, feeling sure of his answer. "We're choosing animals, Billy," she said. "You mustn't worry if you weren't listening."

Billy was silent.

"Were you listening, Billy?"

"Yes."

"And you don't want Zucchini?"

"No."

"I'm surprised," said Miss Pickett. "Do you have a reason?"

"No," said Billy. He was so upset he left without saying good-bye.

Chapter Twenty-one

Trust

Billy ran all the way home, opened the front door with his key, went straight into his room and shut the door.

"I'm no good," he repeated over and over. "I'm the stupidest person that ever lived! I hate myself! I hate myself!"

"How come?" said Emma. She popped out of Billy's closet, carrying a small rubber ball with a slightly purple tinge.

"Get out of here!" shouted Billy. "Who said you could come in my room?"

"Did I scare you?" asked Emma.

"No," said Billy.

"How come I didn't scare you?" Emma asked. She was clearly disappointed.

"Get out!" Billy shouted. "Get out, now!"

"O.K.," said Emma. "I was only testing your Super Ball. If you were ever wondering if it glows in the dark, it does."

"I know it does," said Billy. "Who said you could play with it anyway?"

"It was in the living room. I didn't think you'd mind."

"I mind."

"I'm sorry."

"All right. Now, leave me alone."

"Do you want to come to my Halloween party?"

"No."

"It's gonna be great! Tracy and I are making scary decorations. Cats and bones and witches and ghosts and spiders. Uggh! I'm warning you! And Tracy's bringing a record of spooky sounds. There's gonna also be The Web of Night. Wanna know what that is?"

"No."

"I'm tying string to all the furniture in a certain room, and we're gonna turn out all the lights and make everyone go in. They're gonna fall down, boy!"

"Sounds great," said Billy.

"Oh, yeah!" said Emma, thinking he was serious. "You should really come. I'm gonna be the great chicken monster."

"I know."

"Well, I am, and One-Day Service is coming. I'm gonna make the tiniest costume for him. He's gonna be a ghost."

"Fine," said Billy. "Now, leave me alone."

"Why do you hate yourself?"

"Never mind."

"But why? You're not so bad."

"It's none of your business."

"All right," said Emma. "Do you want your Super Ball?"

"You can have it," said Billy.

"Thanks," said Emma. "Thank you very much. You can be a very nice person sometimes." She turned and started out. "Do you want your door closed?" she called back over her shoulder.

"Yes," said Billy.

"I hope you feel better," said Emma. Then she closed the door.

That night, Zucchini had a talk with Arnold. He had opened Arnold's cage, and they were sitting on the window ledge, looking out over the Texaco gas station.

"You can't trust anybody," said Zucchini. "I know that now."

"Some you can," said the crow. "Not many though."

"I thought he was my friend," said Zucchini.

"People have their ways," said the crow.

"If I can't trust Billy, who can I trust?"

"I don't know," said Arnold. "Yourself, I guess."

"I'm leaving as soon as I can," said Zucchini. "I want to get away."

"I understand," said the crow.

"Priscilla should be around soon. I'll open your cage, and then I'll leave."

"I'm much obliged," said the crow.

"How long have you been here?" asked Zucchini.

"It's going on two years now," answered the crow.

"That's a long time to be in a cage," said Zucchini.

"That's right," said Arnold.

"And they're waiting for you on Staten Island?"

"That's right."

"That's a long time to wait," said Zucchini. "Don't take this the wrong way, but have you ever wondered if they're still waiting? I mean two years is a long time."

"I've wondered," said Arnold.

Zucchini expected Arnold to say something more, but he didn't.

"I'll let you out," said Zucchini. "You can trust me."

At seven-thirty the next morning, Priscilla opened the door to the zoo.

"Heigh-ho," she said to herself. "Here I go again." She set down her pail and went out to collect her mops and brooms.

Zucchini was sitting on the chair by the door. He hadn't slept all night, what with sadness over Billy and nervousness over his impending journey. When he saw Priscilla, he crouched very low in his chair, trying to make himself small and hard to notice. Priscilla headed back out for her equipment, and Zucchini peered around the edge of the door. He could see through Miss Pickett's office and right out into the hall.

Go! he thought. This is my chance!

He leaped from the chair, hurried through Miss Pickett's office, out into the hallway, down the ramp, out the back door, around the building and stared at the rising sun.

There it is, he thought. Then he turned and headed the other way, moving west on Ninety-second Street.

When Arnold woke up and found Zucchini gone, a shiver ran through his body.

Chapter Twenty-two

Marsha's Bag

Zucchini turned right on Park Avenue and hurried along unnoticed by taxi drivers, ladies in hats, children with school books, men with briefcases, doormen and dogs. He saw a boy who looked like Billy, the same light hair and large eyes, but as the boy got closer, it was clearly someone else.

I'll never see him again, thought Zucchini. I have to get used to that.

At Ninety-sixth Street Zucchini stopped to rest. A man came out of the building on the corner carrying two suitcases. He wore a green crew-neck sweater, and a camera hung around his neck on a leather strap.

"Forget the shampoo, Marsha," he called back over his shoulder. "They have stores in Oklahoma."

Oklahoma! thought Zucchini. Did he say Oklahoma?

The man set the suitcases down on the sidewalk as a lady followed him out of the building. She had dark hair, wore slacks and carried a large canvas bag with a loaf of sourdough bread sticking out the top.

"I know they have stores in Oklahoma. I know that, Herb," she was saying as she joined the man by the suitcases. "I just hope we can get a cab. They never want to go to the airport."

She set down her canvas bag and ran into the street, waving and shouting and leaping up and down. "Taxi! Taxi!" she screamed.

Jump into the bag! thought Zucchini. Do it! This is your chance!

"Taxi! Taxi!" screamed Marsha.

"He sees us, Marsha," said the man. He seemed embarrassed.

A yellow taxi pulled to a screeching halt.

Now! thought Zucchini. It's now or never!

He took a running leap and jumped into Marsha's bag.

"Kennedy Airport," said Marsha. Then she ran back to get her bag.

"I just came from there," said the driver.

"Well, you're going back," said Marsha. She opened the cab door and got in. "Come on, Herb."

"I'll just put these in the trunk," he mumbled.

Herb approached with the suitcases.

"What do you want from me?" said the driver. "They're backed up to the Hutch."

"We have time," said Marsha.

"What about me? I gotta come back, you know."

"You'll have to deal with it," said Marsha.

"Two hours empty on the Van Wyck. They never think of that."

"It's your job," said Marsha. "Get in, Herb."

Herb put the cases in the back and got in. The driver heaved a great sigh, flipped his flag and pulled off.

I'm on my way, thought Zucchini as he settled down next to the sourdough bread. I'm leaving Billy, but I'll find where I belong. I've got to!

The motion of the taxi made him sleepy, and soon he fell asleep.

When Zucchini woke up, he was at American Airlines check-in.

"Take that off the belt, Herb!" Marsha was saying. "That's my carry-on!"

Zucchini heard rattling noises and felt the sensation of being

TAXI

swept along at great speed as Marsha's bag traveled along the conveyor belt just behind the ticket lady with severe allergies.

"I'll get it," said the lady through her nose, and Zucchini felt himself being lifted high into the air.

"Thank you," said Marsha. She grabbed the bag.

The lady blew her nose.

"You should do something for that cold," said Marsha.

The ticket lady sneezed. "Allergies," she said.

"Whatever," said Marsha.

The ticket lady sneezed again.

"Nothing helps in October," she said. "That's Gate Nine, boarding at ten-fifteen."

"Let's go, Herb," said Marsha, and they started off to find Gate Nine.

This can't be Oklahoma, thought Zucchini as he peered out over the top of Marsha's bag. It looks like the ASPCA, only bigger, more people, more noise. I don't like it. This can't be where I belong. *What's that??*

Up ahead, Zucchini had spotted airport security. People were lining up, and hand luggage was being piled onto a large moving belt which passed through a big machine.

What *is* that? I don't want to go in there!

"Hand check this please," said Herb to the robust security lady in the peaked cap. He held out his camera.

"It won't hurt your film," said the lady, as if for the thousandth time.

What won't? thought Zucchini. I'd better get out of this bag.

"Yes, it will," said Herb. "I go through this every time I travel."

"Not *this* machine," said the lady. She seemed proud.

"Hand check it for him, would you please?" said Marsha. "Just hand check it."

"It won't hurt the film," the lady said stubbornly. Her uniform was too tight, bringing on discomfort and irritability. The line of people was backing up.

"We have a plane to catch," said Marsha, "in case that comes as a surprise."

The lady grabbed the camera angrily from Herb and passed it to the thin young man behind her.

"Hand check," she said.

Let me out of here! thought Zucchini, peering past the sourdough bread at the large X-ray machine.

Marsha put her bag on the belt and glanced at an advertisement on the wall. KNOW *THE* THINGS TO TALK ABOUT. READ *TIME* MAGAZINE, said the ad.

Now's my chance! thought Zucchini, and he jumped out of the bag just before it was enveloped in the monstrous machine.

The security lady was already dealing with the next in line, an oval-faced man with a bag of rotten fruit.

"They won't let *that* on," she said, pointing to the fruit.

The man stared blankly into space. Along with the fruit he carried a broom and a portable Sony TV.

"Do you speak English?" she continued.

Zucchini leaped off the belt and scurried about the feet of the crowd of passengers. Marsha picked up her bag when it came out of the machine, and Herb retrieved his camera.

"What gate was it?" asked Marsha.

"Nine," said Herb.

I'd better follow them, thought Zucchini. They're going to Oklahoma. They must know the way.

At Gate Nine there was a long line of people having their tickets checked.

"Would you like a window seat?" The young man put the question to a gray-haired lady wearing white socks and carrying a badminton racket.

"I don't look out," she whispered confidentially.

"Attention all passengers," said the loudspeaker. "Your Astroliner Flight Number Three to Oklahoma City is now ready for boarding. Please have your boarding passes ready as you prepare to board the aircraft. Have a pleasant flight and thank you for choosing American."

"Have you got the stubs?" said Marsha.

"Boarding passes," said Herb.

"Whatever," said Marsha, and Zucchini followed them down the long tunnellike boarding ramp.

What is this? he wondered. Where am I going? It looks like the rodent house.

"Good morning, sir," said the stewardess when Herb reached the door of the plane. "May I see your boarding pass, please?"

Herb showed her the passes.

"All righty then, fine," said the stewardess. She looked like she'd been awakened in the night and asked to smile for reasons she didn't understand. "You'll be in our luxury coach section today." She seemed delighted.

"Where's that?" said Herb.

"Just proceed to the rear of the aircraft," said the stewardess. "Good morning," she continued with great cheerfulness to a short man with a plastic plant. "May I stow that in the forward cabin?"

The man seemed reluctant.

"Push through, Herb," said Marsha. "We're in the back."

What is this place? thought Zucchini. It's a nightmare.

He followed Herb and Marsha toward the rear of the plane, getting stepped on several times.

"Here we are," said Marsha. "T2 and 3."

They sat down, and Zucchini crawled in under Herb's seat.

I hope they know what they're doing, he thought.

After an hour's delay, many announcements, much changing of seats, hanging of coats and passing of magazines, they were ready for takeoff. Zucchini was terrified by the loud rush of the engines, but when they leveled off, he soon got used to the feeling of flight.

I'm on my way, he thought. At least, I hope I am.

He huddled beneath the seat, wondering where he was, where he was going, if he'd ever find his home, if he'd know it when he got there. Then he thought of Billy and was filled with sadness. He felt totally alone, like the time way back in the rodent house when they separated him from his mother.

Chapter Twenty-three

Peanut Butter Cookies

At that very moment, Billy was in the kitchen with Emma, making a batch of peanut butter cookies. He wanted to bring Zucchini a present, something to make up for the day before. Not choosing Zucchini for the class report was bad enough, but leaving without saying good-bye, that was worse. He knew he had upset his friend. He didn't know how much.

"Let's pretend we're cookers," said Emma.

"O.K.," said Billy.

"Can I take them out of the oven?" asked Emma.

"You'll burn yourself," said Billy, rolling up the sleeves of his pajamas. He had a sore throat and was spending the day inside. "You better let me do it."

"Why?"

"Because you'll burn yourself."

"I want to do it."

"Do you want to burn yourself?"

"No."

"Then let me do it."

Billy put on the protective gloves and pulled the cookie sheet out of the oven.

"When can we eat them?" asked Emma.

"As soon as they're cool."

"I want to eat one now."

"Do you want to burn yourself?"

"No."

"Then wait."

"Will we have a stove in our new house?"

"We're not going to move to a new house."

"We might," said Emma. "Dad said. Will there be a stove?"

"You always have a stove," said Billy, "but we're not moving."

"What do you want me to make you with my rocks?" said Emma. The tumbler was still going strong, scraping and grinding as it spun. It often kept Billy awake. "Daddy's getting cuff links, and I'm making Mommy a very beautiful pin, so what do you want?"

"I don't care."

"You could have a tie clip."

"Fine. But I think that tumbler's broken."

"It's not," said Emma. "It's apposed to sound like that."

"Supposed," said Billy, "but I think it's broken."

"Not for a minute," said Emma. "You'll see."

The cookies were cool, and they divided them up, saving one for each of their parents. Emma began eating hers right away.

"What are you doing?" she asked when she saw Billy wrap three of his cookies in waxed paper.

"I'm saving these for Zucchini."

"You're not going to eat them?"

"Not these."

"Wow," said Emma, her eyes staring with wonder. "You're crazy."

The next morning Billy's sore throat was better. He put the peanut butter cookies in the right front pocket of his blue jeans and headed for the ASPCA. He was glad it was Saturday, and he didn't have to take the cookies to school. The kids would ask what was making that big bulge in his pocket, and if he told them it was cookies someone might take them. There were a couple of kids who would do a mean thing like that. Brian would and so would Mike.

As Billy passed through the front door of the ASPCA, he took the cookies out of his pocket. He could smell the peanut butter through the waxed paper wrap.

Zucchini will like these, he thought as he passed the information lady, perched high on her stool. Up the ramp he went, down the third-floor hallway, through Miss Pickett's office and into the zoo. Miss Pickett was standing over by the window.

"Hello, Billy," she said.

Billy didn't answer. He stared at the empty cage.

"He's been gone since yesterday," said Miss Pickett.

Billy's nose began to itch, and he knew he was about to cry. He didn't like to cry in front of people, especially anybody who wasn't his mother, but he couldn't help it. Tears streamed down his face as he stood in front of the empty cage, holding the peanut butter cookies meant for his friend.

"What's the matter?" asked Emma when she opened the front door. She was holding a pumpkin, freshly carved, with three triangular eyes and jagged teeth. "Were you crying?"

Billy just walked inside and sat down on the couch. Emma followed.

"Look at this pumpkin," she said. "Mom helped me, but I mostly did it. It's going in the window with a candle and everybody's gonna be scared."

Billy was trying to hold back his tears, but he couldn't manage it. He rubbed his eyes, hoping his sister wouldn't notice.

"What's wrong?" asked Emma.

Billy didn't answer.

"Whatcha crying for?"

Billy kept crying, kept rubbing his eyes.

"Mama's working in the studio. Do you want me to get her?"

"Zucchini's gone," said Billy.

"Where'd he go?"

"I don't know."

"Maybe he went for a walk."

"He didn't go for any walk."

"Maybe robbers took him."

Billy started to cry again.

"Don't cry," said Emma. "Wanna see my slime with eyeballs?"

"No," said Billy.

"It's for party favors," said Emma. "It's running, dripping slime that's green, and inside there's bloodshot eyeballs. They're not real though. They're only plastic."

"I don't want to hear about it."

"Don't worry about the ferret. He'll be all right."

"I keep thinking he might be hurt. Maybe he got hit by a car, or he could be just lost, and he could be looking for his way back, and maybe he doesn't know how to find it. Maybe he'll starve to death."

"I hope not," said Emma.

"He was weak and sick already," said Billy. "I hope he doesn't die."

"I don't like dying," said Emma. "Tracy fed her guinea pig so much it exploded."

"That's not true," said Billy.

"Tracy told me."

"It's not true, and it's not funny."

"Don't be mad."

At dinnertime there was more bad news.

"I'm sorry about the ferret," Billy's stepfather said, "but here's something to cheer you up. It's definite! We're moving to the country. We'll be in our new house by the end of next month."

"Will we live in a cave?" asked Emma. She had just seen a Tarzan movie on TV.

"A cave?" asked Mrs. Ferguson. "What gives you that idea?"

"I was just wondering what kind of country it will be and will there be caves."

"No caves," said Mr. Ferguson. "Houses. Houses and grass and trees and fresh air. I wouldn't be surprised if Billy could have a pet."

"I don't want one," said Billy.

"You may feel differently after a month," said his mother.

"I won't," said Billy. He couldn't eat any supper. He just stared at his food and pushed it around his plate with his fork.

Chapter Twenty-four

Central Park Zoo

Each morning before school Billy would stop by the ASPCA to see if there was any news. On the third day Miss Pickett had an idea.

"The Central Park Zoo has acquired a new ferret," she said. She sat behind her desk, wearing her hat and fingering her ring of keys. "We received a bulletin regarding new acquisitions in yesterday's mail."

Billy's heart began to race.

Don't let me get my hopes up, he thought. I'll only be disappointed.

"I telephoned right away," continued Miss Pickett, "but the woman in charge was out sick. I spoke to a man who said he thought the ferret was at least two years old, but he wasn't sure. It is a male, though, and it came in this week, so it's worth a try."

"It's probably not him."

"Perhaps not," said Miss Pickett, "but why not stop by after school today and find out. We may have a happy surprise."

Billy said nothing. He was sitting in the corner, slumped down in his chair, staring at his sneakers.

"I know it's hard for you to question strangers," Miss Pickett continued, "but it just might be our ferret." She got up and went over to check on Arnold. She had brought his cage into her office. She was worried about him, because he had stopped eating. "What do you say?"

"All right," Billy said at last.

After school Billy walked over to Fifth Avenue and took the bus to Sixty-fourth Street. He could see the balloon man selling his balloons and the pretzel man selling his pretzels as he got off the bus and headed down the steps to the zoo. He turned left by the hot dog man and went under the clock with the musical animals that danced every hour on the hour. Squirrels scurried back and forth across the path asking for nuts and Cracker Jack, but Billy had no time for them. He had to see the ferret before they closed the zoo.

At the monkey house the orangutan was sitting on her rubber tire, eating Italian ice from a paper cup. She licked the ice very slowly and with great care. When she was finished she ate the cup.

Billy reached the children's section, paid his money to enter and headed through the glass doors. On the right was a row of pens with chickens and rabbits you could pat and, at the end, an incubator for baby chicks. You could look through the glass and watch them hatch.

The children's zoo was crowded, and Billy inched his way past babies in strollers, children with balloons and parents with glazed expressions. When he got to the ferret's cage he stopped. A sign hung on the front of the cage.

FERRET

The cage was empty.

They must have just taken it out, he thought. There's its log and its water dish and its grain and vegetables. They haven't even cleaned the cage, or set it up for another animal. I wonder what happened.

He started back through the exit doors, then stopped. There was a very small man sitting in the glass booth by the exit. Slowly, Billy approached him.

"Where's the ferret?" Billy asked.

"What?" said the man. He squinted his eyes and looked up. His skin was all wrinkled, like a prune.

"Where's the ferret?" asked Billy, louder this time.

"No know," said the man. "No speak." He pointed back over his shoulder to a door marked NO ADMITTANCE.

I can't knock on a door that says NO ADMITTANCE, thought Billy. That means no going in.

The door opened suddenly and a stout man stood behind it. He had a crew cut and wore a bow tie on a white shirt that said ASSISTANT MANAGER across the front. In his shirt pocket was a row of automatic pencils.

"That's enough for today, Gladys," he called out over Billy's head. "Put him in."

Billy turned and saw Gladys, a black woman, sitting some distance away with a large rabbit.

"I don't mind," shouted Gladys, and she picked up the rabbit.

"You want something, young fellow?" asked the man.

"No," said Billy.

"You're not lost, are you?"

"No."

"Looking for the rest room?"

"No," said Billy. "Where's the ferret?"

"What?" asked the man. He looked confused.

"The ferret," said Billy.

"Ferret," said the man as if reminding himself. "Through the glass doors on your left."

"It's not there," said Billy.

"Oh, that's right," said the man. He seemed distracted. He breathed through his mouth, and his shirt was a size too small. "That's the new one. It'll be out in a few days."

"Where is it?" said Billy.

"In the back."

"Why is it in the back?"

"It wasn't eating its dinner, young fellow."

"Oh," said Billy.

"You always eat your dinner, don't you?"

"If I'm hungry."

"Sure you do," said the man. "There's a good boy."

"Can I see it?" said Billy.

"Not now," said the man. "It's in the back."

Billy's heart sank. Maybe the ferret really was Zucchini. He had to see him. Why didn't the man understand?

"I have to see him!" Billy blurted out. He was surprised at the sound of his own voice. He hadn't expected to shout.

"Patience, young fellow," said the man. He patted Billy on the shoulder. "Enjoy the zoo."

"I can't," said Billy. "I have to see the ferret! I had a ferret, and I lost it. I have to see if it's mine."

"Well, why didn't you say so, son?" said the man. "We aim to please. Come with me."

The man led Billy down a long corridor and into a small, brightly lit room. A young woman in white overalls was feeding a baby monkey, and to her right, in a cage by the window, was a ferret, an adorable ferret, with a curious expression, bright eyes, and a twitching nose. Billy stared for several minutes before he spoke.

"He'd like some milk," said Billy.

"I was considering that," said the woman feeding the monkey, "but they shouldn't have too much."

"I know," said Billy. "Just a little."

"So, young fellow," said the man, "have we got your ferret?"

"No," said Billy.

"I didn't think so," said the man. "But good luck to you. I hope you find him."

Later that night Billy sat with his mother in the kitchen. His stepfather was working late, and Emma had been put to bed. She had had her Halloween party that night, and things were still in disarray. Strings hung off furniture (remnants of The Web of Night), party favors were strewn about, and here and there were candy wrappers, paper skeletons, and discarded bubble gum cards. Billy and his mother sat at the small kitchen table drinking hot chocolate and playing crazy eights. Billy's mother had suggested the game, which was Billy's favorite. She could see he was upset and hoped to cheer him up. She figured she'd complete the cleaning in the morning.

"Clubs," she said, placing an eight of hearts face up on the table.

Billy didn't respond.

"Your turn," said his mother.

"I don't want to play anymore," said Billy. "I'm tired."

"I'll play," said Emma. She appeared suddenly from behind the kitchen door, wearing her nightgown and clutching a large stuffed frog.

"What are you doing up?" asked her mother.

"I can't sleep," said Emma. "There's things in my room."

"What things?" her mother asked.

"I don't know," said Emma. "Creepy. Very creepy things."

"There are no creepy things in your room," said her mother. "Now go back to bed."

"Yes, there are," said Emma. "They may be alligators. They're making banging noises, and I get scared."

While his mother went in to check on the alligators, Billy poured himself some more hot chocolate. His trip to the zoo had left him more depressed than ever. There was no hope of finding Zucchini. He was sure of that. Zucchini was probably dead.

"I think I'll have some more hot chocolate, too," said his mother, returning to the kitchen. "Your ferret may still come back," she continued, "but if he doesn't, it's really not the end of the world. Someone may have taken him in. He may be perfectly safe."

"I doubt it," said Billy.

"I'm proud of the way you went to the zoo today and asked

the people for help," said his mother. "I know it wasn't easy."

"It's not fair," said Billy. "I did something hard like that, and it doesn't even help."

"Maybe it will," said his mother.

The hot chocolate was good, soothing to Billy's stomach. He took several long sips, then sat, staring into his cup.

"Tomorrow's another day," said his mother. It was one of the few things she said that made no sense. He wished she wouldn't say it. He knew tomorrow was another day. He also knew what she meant, that something good might happen, but something bad might happen too.

He gave his mother a hug and went to bed.

Chapter Twenty-five

Shopping Mall

Zucchini was heading west on Route 40. He had spent the last three days at the American Airlines oversized baggage area in Oklahoma City. Marsha's durable tan Samsonite suitcase had been lost in transit. So, after waiting one and a half hours by the baggage claim belt, she and Herb had been forced to go to the service area and place their complaint. Zucchini had climbed out of Marsha's canvas bag at that location amidst a sea of cigarette smoke and accusations by desperate and weary travelers.

"What do you mean it was sent to Hong Kong?"

"If this is what you do best, I'd hate to see what else you do."

"What have you done with my dog?"

"You dare to wear your 'Number One' button and misplace my Gucci?"

"They have no room for the luggage. They throw it off the plane."

"It's not just American. They're all the same. Take a trip, lose a bag."

Zucchini had attempted to leave, but instead had wandered into the oversized baggage area and was trapped behind a tower of crates by the rear door. He had hurried into an empty crate to avoid getting crushed by a fast-moving baggage tram, and before he knew it, a whole tower of crates had been stacked in front of him, and there was no way out.

There Zucchini spent three of the darkest days of his life. No food. No water. No trace of hope. The tiny ferret huddled in the corner of the empty crate, knowing the end had surely come. I've come so far for this, he thought. I hoped it would be different.

Each day he became more and more frightened, more and more certain that he was about to die; but on the third day, miraculously and without warning, the crates were unstacked, and Zucchini was discovered by a clean-shaven, efficient young baggage representative, who immediately reported him to his service manager. The service manager recommended that they feed Zucchini, give him water and put a tracer on him right away.

Zucchini had been grateful for the food (Purina Sea Nip Dinner) and the water, but as soon as he had eaten, he spotted an open door. The baggage representative had neglected to lock Zucchini's cage carefully enough, and Zucchini had little difficulty in managing the tiny latch. He escaped the baggage area, darted around the edge of the airfield and was soon heading west on Route 40.

Treffinger said west, thought Zucchini, staring at the late afternoon sun, so this is the right direction, but it doesn't look like the prairies. I guess they're farther up.

On he went. He passed many gas stations, Airport Travel Inns, billboards and highway interchanges. Large diesel trucks roared past, noisy jets thundered in overhead on their landing patterns, motorcycles, buses and passenger cars zoomed past. Zucchini felt very small and very lonely. Where am I? he thought. What will become of me? Why did I decide to make this journey? Was it all a mistake?

Off to the side was a rather more peaceful side road with a few trees, and Zucchini decided to take it.

Maybe I have my directions a little wrong, he thought. This looks more like it.

It was dusk now and getting cold. He passed a firehouse on his left and a church on his right. He was tired, but he wanted to continue.

The sooner I find those prairies the better, he thought. I have to keep on.

Night came, and Zucchini continued. He passed schools and stores, gas stations and factories. Then he climbed a large hill. When he got to the top and looked down, he saw a large shopping mall. It was after midnight, and the mall was deserted. The enormous parking lot spread out before him with lights lighting up the windows and signs of the various stores.

Could this be it? he thought. It's open. And big. And look at the lights, all different colors. He stared at the neon lights blinking the words ZAP ZAP JEANS IN A MINUTE.

Have I found it?

Very slowly Zucchini made his way down the hill.

It's quiet. It's open.

He sniffed the air.

What's the smell?

He was only yards away from HUNG LUCK FOW'S CHINESE RESTAURANT ("Take it out or eat it here"). Their evening's leftovers filled two trash cans by the rear door.

Are those the smells I was looking for? They don't seem exactly as I remember them, but they sure smell good.

Zucchini climbed up on one of the garbage cans, dislodged the cover of the other can and had a sumptuous dinner of egg rolls, spare ribs, crispy noodles and pork fried rice. Then he fell asleep.

When Zucchini woke up it was nearly six. He stretched and blinked his eyes in the early morning sun.

What a nice sleep, he thought. He climbed back into the garbage can and had some more noodles and another half an egg roll. Then he looked around. The early morning light was beautiful. It streamed down through the mist, lighting the deserted parking lot.

Can this be it? thought the tiny ferret. Am I home?

He began walking, hurrying to take in all the sights. He passed many shops. FAST FAT-BURGERS ("Biggest burgers in town"), SHOE KING BOB'S ("Buy a pair, get a pair free"), TAB'S PORK GYROS ("Meat on a spear"), THE BLASTED EARDRUM ("Sound in the next dimension"), and many more. Zucchini couldn't read the signs, but the shops looked colorful, exciting.

This looks like it, he thought, but where are the other ferrets? I'm the only one here.

Slowly, the mall began to fill up with people. Shops opened for the day and cars began to crowd the parking lot. Zucchini stopped to sun himself in front of MARIO'S GRAB-A-PIZZA as two enormous delivery trucks pulled up by the supermarket next door.

"Back her up, Jim," shouted the A&P man, directing the trucker at the wheel.

Two boys on skateboards whizzed past, nearly running Zucchini over.

This doesn't seem right, he thought. It's getting noisy and crowded. Something's wrong.

Suddenly a blast of noise echoed through the parking lot. "I'M GONNA GET YOU, BABY," shrieked a raucous disco group. Drums pounded, guitars wailed, and Zucchini hid for safety under a Ford station wagon. THE BLASTED EARDRUM record shop had opened for the day.

More and more cars pulled into parking spaces, and people began milling about, rushing blankly to complete their day's errands. Exhaust fumes dulled the delicious smells from HUNG LUCK FOW'S, the disco group overpowered the chirping of birds, and Zucchini knew for sure that this was not his home.

Those noodles were nice, he thought, but there's more to life than noodles. I have to find my home. That's right and true. It's the only way for me.

Chapter Twenty-six

Nine-Banded Armadillo

Zucchini traveled long and hard all through the day. At three that afternoon he passed a schoolhouse just as the children were being dismissed. One of the boys looked a lot like Billy, and Zucchini stopped and stared.

My friend, he thought. I miss you.

It was nearing dusk when Zucchini reached a wide river.

How beautiful, he thought. It looks like that place I went to with Billy where we ate those tasty treats from the man with the wagon.

Zucchini stopped and took a deep breath and stared at the setting sun.

I'm almost home, he thought. I'm almost there.

Just then he saw a strange sight on the surface of the river. A tiny pink snoutlike thing was moving slowly toward him.

It looks like a nose, thought Zucchini, but whose nose?

The nose moved steadily closer, and then up from the water beneath it rose a small, piglike animal with the shell of a turtle.

What is that? thought Zucchini.

It was an armadillo. It was about the size of a house cat, with a shell covering its back and tail. The shell was mottled dark brown and ridged by nine bands. The eyes were set in a fringe of long lashes, and the long, slender nose was tipped with pink.

When the armadillo saw Zucchini, he was startled and bounced straight up into the air like a jack-in-the-box. Then he landed on the ground, frozen in fear.

"I won't hurt you," said Zucchini. "I'm a baby ferret."

The armadillo appeared to relax a bit. He stared at Zucchini for a moment before he spoke.

"You startled me," he said.

"You startled me too," said Zucchini. "At first all I saw of you was your nose. It was alarming."

"I didn't mean it to be," said the armadillo, "but there it is."

"I know," said Zucchini. "It doesn't alarm me when I see it on your face with your head and the rest of you. It was just seeing it move by itself across the river that gave me a scare."

"Sorry," said the armadillo. "That wasn't my intention. Where you bound for?"

"The prairies," said Zucchini.

"I see," said the armadillo. He sat down and Zucchini noticed his bare and hairless underside.

"By the way," said Zucchini. "Do you know if I'm heading in the right direction?"

"You are," said the armadillo. "You're approaching the panhandle."

"What's that?" asked Zucchini.

"An area," said the armadillo. "It's nice, and it has prairies."

"Am I far away?" asked Zucchini.

"Not in the least," said the armadillo, "but I'd suggest camping here for the night, if I may be so bold."

"Oh, you may," said Zucchini.

"Good," said the armadillo. "Camp here for the night and set out in the morning. I'd say you could reach the prairies by late afternoon."

"That's wonderful," said Zucchini. "My dream come true! Have you ever been there?"

"I have," said the armadillo.

"Is it beautiful?"

"Yes."

"And peaceful?"

"Yes."

"Are there other ferrets there?"

"Yes."

"That's it!" said Zucchini. "Thank you for your help!"

"I'm happy to do what I can," said the armadillo. "I seldom get the chance."

"Why not?"

"I look funny."

"That's true," said Zucchini, "but you're so nice that soon you forget. I forgot already."

"I appreciate the sentiment," said the armadillo. "Are you hungry?"

"Oh, yes," said Zucchini."

"What do you favor?" asked the armadillo.

"Favor?"

"What do you like?"

"I'm not particular."

"I've got a stash in my burrow, if you'll come with me. I've got some grasshoppers, roaches, fire ants and maybe a spider."

"Do you have any carrots?"

"No," said the armadillo.

"That's all right," said Zucchini. "Grasshoppers will be fine."

Zucchini followed the armadillo to its nearby burrow and waited for him to bring up the food. They sat by the river eating and resting and watching the moon rise over the deep water.

"I admire you," said the armadillo after a lengthy silence.

"Why me?" said Zucchini. "I'm young and inexperienced and just getting started."

"You're following your dream," said the armadillo. "Not many have the courage."

"I hope I find it," said Zucchini.

"You will," said the armadillo.

"How far would you say the prairies are from here?" asked Zucchini. He was starting on his third grasshopper.

"About fifteen miles," said the armadillo.

"Fifteen?" said Zucchini.

"About fifteen," said the armadillo. "As the crow flies."

Zucchini stopped chewing. His tiny body went numb.

"Are you all right?" asked the armadillo.

Zucchini said nothing. He sat motionless, his head held high.

"Something wrong with the food?" asked the armadillo.

"Crow," said Zucchini.

"What's that?" said the armadillo.

"Crow," said Zucchini.

"Crow what?" said the armadillo.

"I forgot," said Zucchini.

"Forgot what?" said the armadillo. "Care for a beetle?"

"Arnold," said Zucchini. "I forgot all about him."

"Who's Arnold?" asked the armadillo.

"A friend of mine," said Zucchini. "I left him in New York City. I promised to let him out, and I forgot."

"He'll manage," said the armadillo, "they always do. We like to think we're indispensable, but it's never the case. Have a beetle."

"I have to go back," said Zucchini.

"I wouldn't," said the armadillo.

"I promised him," said Zucchini.

"He'll forget about it," said the armadillo.

"I won't," said Zucchini.

"Sure you will," said the armadillo. "You have a dream. You better go after it. Talk to one who didn't."

"I have to go back," said Zucchini.

"You'll regret it," said the armadillo. "Time waits for no one. You won't get a second chance."

"That may be," said Zucchini, "but I promised my friend."

Chapter Twenty-seven

Moving

Billy's apartment was stacked high with packing crates. They would be moving in ten days, and they were doing all the packing themselves. Billy's mother sat on the floor wearing her blue jeans and a blue work shirt. She looked tired, which was the way she'd been looking since they started packing.

"I never know what to do with things like this," she was saying. She held up a ring of old keys, two hairpins and a button. "Should I pack them, or shouldn't I pack them, or if I should pack them, where should I pack them?" She was talking partly to herself and partly to her husband who stood nearby packing books.

"Don't pack them," he said. "Throw them out." That was always his answer.

"I'm not throwing out my Play-Doh," said Emma, peering into a large barrel. "That stays."

"Be sure it's in a plastic bag," said Mrs. Ferguson. "We don't need that."

"We don't need what?"

"Your Play-Doh all over everything."

Billy was in his room taking the animal pictures off his wall. His mother had said he could leave them up for a while if he wanted to, but he said he didn't care. He'd been saying that a lot since Zucchini left. Just then Emma came in with her yo-yo.

"You wanna see a trick?" she asked.

"No," said Billy.

"You don't have to be grouchy," said Emma. "I just asked."

"I'm busy," said Billy, "and anyway, you can't do any tricks. You always say that, and you never can do any tricks. You just let it go down to the bottom of the string and hang. It's always the same."

"That's not true," said Emma, "and I'll tell you one thing. Ever since that ferret disappeared you've been the meanest thing."

Billy pulled at a picture, and a big hunk of paint and plaster came off with the Scotch tape. Then he sat down on the bed and began to cry.

"Don't cry," said Emma. "Please don't cry." She went over and hugged him. "Everything's going to be O.K."

The following morning when Billy was getting dressed for school, his stepfather knocked on the door.

"I'll be out in a minute," said Billy. He thought it was Emma.

"It's me," said Mr. Ferguson. "Can I come in?"

"Sure," said Billy. "I didn't know it was you."

Mr. Ferguson came in and sat down next to Billy on the bed.

"Are you O.K.?" he asked. He carried a tennis racquet, which he must have been in the process of packing, because he didn't have his tennis clothes on.

"I'm O.K.," said Billy.

"You seem so unhappy lately. Is there anything I can do?"

"No," said Billy.

"Are you worried about moving, or is it still the ferret?"

"Both, I guess," said Billy.

"I tell you what," said his stepfather. "Here's two things I can think of. When we go, if they haven't found the ferret, we'll leave our address and phone number at the ASPCA, and if he comes back, they can call us and I personally will drive you down from Binghamton to see him."

"What's Binghamton?" asked Emma. She stood in the doorway, licking a frozen juice bar.

"You know," said Mr. Ferguson. "That's where our new house will be, just outside Binghamton. We'll have grass and trees and a backyard. We can put up a swing."

"Will there be spiders?" asked Emma. Her frozen juice bar was dripping down the stick and down to her elbow.

"There might be an occasional spider," said Mr. Ferguson. "There's a few spiders most everywhere."

"Not in my room," said Emma. "I don't go where there's spiders."

"We'll discuss that later," said Mr. Ferguson. "Right now I'm talking to Billy." And he continued, "The other thing, Billy, is if you like, once we get settled, I don't see why we can't have a dog. What do you think?"

"No thanks," said Billy. "I don't want a pet."

Zucchini had left the armadillo's burrow and was approaching the airport in Oklahoma City. He had retraced his steps all the way from the river to the shopping mall, to Route 40, to the rear entrance of the American Airlines oversized baggage area. What followed was surely a miracle. With all thoughts of the prairies behind him, his mind centered only on fulfilling his promise, the tiny ferret went through the oversized baggage area to the baggage service area, through the baggage service area out into the terminal by the baggage claim belts, heard the announcement for the boarding at Gate Nine of Flight Number Seven to New York, went to Gate Nine, boarded the aircraft, flew to New York's John F. Kennedy Airport, got off the plane, followed the passengers out of the terminal to the taxi and bus area, overheard a lady say she was taking the bus to New York City, followed her onto the airport bus, traveled to New York's East Side Airlines Terminal near the river at Thirty-eighth Street, got off the bus, followed the familiar footpath up the river to Ninety-second Street, turned into the back door of the ASPCA, walked past the information lady, up the ramp and sat down in front of Miss Pickett's door. It was after five o'clock, and there Zucchini spent the night.

Early the next morning Priscilla came down the hallway singing "Careless Love." She carried her pail, two mops and a broom.

"Another day, another dollar," she said to herself. She finished her song and set down her pail. Then she got out her keys and opened the door to the office.

Looks nice, thought Zucchini, peering into the familiar room.

Priscilla picked up her pail and headed for the door of the zoo.

"Once I wore my ribbons high," she sang. She set down her pail once more, took out her keys and opened the door of the zoo.

"O.K., you guys," she announced to the animals. "It's me again."

Zucchini followed Priscilla into the zoo. There was Arnold, asleep on his crossbar.

He's still there! thought Zucchini. Now, let Priscilla open the window and leave. I hope she forgot something.

"Let's get some fresh air," said Priscilla, approaching the window. She gripped the metal handles and pulled up the window.

"Forgot my cleanser," she continued. "That's what I did."

I'm dreaming, thought Zucchini. This is too good to be true.

Priscilla turned and left the zoo, and Zucchini hurried to Arnold's cage. He tapped on the window with his tiny paw.

"Arnold! Arnold! Wake up!" he said. "I'm back!"

The crow slowly lifted his head from where he had tucked it, under his wing. He stared straight at Zucchini and blinked as if he too thought he was dreaming.

"It's me, Arnold. I'm back," said Zucchini. He hurried around and opened the back of Arnold's cage. "Please forgive me for forgetting, please, if you can, but you have to go now! Hurry! The window's open! Quick! Before she comes back!"

Arnold blinked a few more times, and then he knew he was awake.

"Hello, Zucchini," he said. "You came back!"

"Yes," said Zucchini. "I came back to let you out. Are you all right? You look very thin."

"I haven't eaten much," said Arnold. "I was discouraged."

"I'm sorry," said Zucchini. "Are you strong enough to fly?"

"I think so," said Arnold. He still seemed half awake.

"You'd better go then," said Zucchini. "She'll be back in a minute."

"I don't know how to thank you properly," said Arnold. "I hope you understand." He took off from the windowsill and headed out over the Texaco gas station.

"Good-bye," said Zucchini, but Arnold didn't hear. He was already high above the East River, moving south on his way to Staten Island.

That's that, thought Zucchini. That's done.

He wandered back into Miss Pickett's office and looked up at her desk.

I'm tired, he thought. I'm so tired.

Then he climbed into his mail bin and went to sleep.

When Billy got back from school his mother was waiting for him downstairs.

"Billy!" she shouted. "Billy!" She ran to greet him. "Miss Pickett called, and Zucchini came back! He's at the ASPCA right now!"

"He's back?" said Billy.

"He's back!" said his mother. She gave him a big hug. "Run! Go! He's there right now!"

Billy turned and ran. He ran across the playground, down the block, through the front door of the ASPCA, up the ramp, down the third-floor hallway and into Miss Pickett's office. There was his ferret, peering out over the edge of the outgoing-mail bin!

Billy stood very still. His eyes filled with tears. Slowly, he moved to Zucchini. He reached out a hand, and let Zucchini sniff it with his nose.

"He came back," said Miss Pickett. She was crying too. "A wild animal returning to a cage. I've never seen it."

Billy picked up Zucchini and held him close.
"I love you," he said through his tears.

A week later Zucchini was heading north. It was a five-hour drive to Binghamton, and Zucchini rode the whole way on Billy's lap. He didn't mind the long trip. He was home already.